Women *of the* Gold Rush

Women *of the* Gold Rush

"The New Penelope" and Other Stories

Frances Fuller Victor
Edited with Introduction by Ida Rae Egli

HEYDAY BOOKS
BERKELEY, CALIFORNIA

© 1998 by Ida Rae Egli

Library of Congress Cataloging-in-Publication Data:

Victor, Frances Fuller, 1826–1902.
    Women of the Gold Rush: "The new Penelope" and other stories / Frances Fuller Victor; edited with introduction by Ida Rae Egli.
      p. cm.
    Contents: The new Penelope—How Jack Hastings sold his mine—Sam Rice's romance—An old fool—Miss Jorgensen.
    ISBN 1-890771-03-1
    1. Frontier and pioneer life—California—Fiction. 2. California—social life and customs—Fiction. 3. Frontier and pioneer life—Oregon—Fiction. 4. Oregon—Social life and customs—Fiction. 5. California—Gold discoveries—Fiction. 6. Women pioneers—California—Fiction. 7. Oregon—Gold discoveries—Fiction. 8. Women pioneers—Oregon—Fiction. I. Egli Ida Rae, 1946–. II. Title.
PS3129.V57A6   1998
813'.4—dc21
                                      98-17753
                                        CIP

Cover Design: Rebecca LeGates
Interior Design/Production: Rebecca LeGates
Printing and Binding: McNaughton & Gunn, Saline, MI

Front cover photo: courtesy of Utah State Historical Society
Back cover photo: Frances Fuller Victor, courtesy of the Society of California Pioneers

Orders, inquiries, and correspondence should be addressed to:
    Heyday Books
    P. O. Box 9145
    Berkeley, CA 94709
    510/549-3564, Fax 510/549-1889
    heyday@heydaybooks.com

Printed in the United States of America

10 9 8 7 6 5 4 3 2 1

CONTENTS

ACKNOWLEDGMENTS

Researching and editing the fiction of Frances Fuller Victor was a pleasure. Since including her work in *No Rooms of Their Own: Women Writers of Early California, 1849-1869*, I have wanted to focus on Victor's fiction alone, especially "The New Penelope." So my inspiration for this book came from Frances Fuller Victor herself. But all else was a collaborative effort. I am especially grateful to Jim Martin, who spent fifteen years researching Victor's biography, as he was so impressed by her writings that he could not allow her life and work to go undocumented. His *A Bit of a Blue: The Life and Work of Frances Fuller Victor* provided me with a boon of biographical and historical information. To some degree, too, George Rathmell's new publication, *Realms of Gold: The Colorful Writers of San Francisco, 1850-1950*, gave me good background material and details about San Francisco when Victor was writing there.

Carol Idler, at the Santa Rosa Junior College library, was extraordinarily helpful in procuring publications through library loan, as were the librarians at U.C. Berkeley's Bancroft Library and the California Historical Society library on Mission Street in San Francisco. I also need to thank my friend Terry Popp, who helped refine the text, as well as my coworkers in the English department at Santa Rosa Junior College, who endured my months of fatigue while working on this publication.

Clearly, the book would never have been printed were it not for the faith and confidence of Malcolm Margolin, publisher of Heyday Books, whose integrity in publishing California history, Native American history, and early California literature is unsurpassed. At Heyday as well, Julianna Fleming, Danny Noble, and Rebecca LeGates have worked to produce this book so that it could be published in a year when it is so significant, that of the sesquicentennial anniversary of the California gold rush.

Finally, I must address the patience, unflagging emotional support, and physical caretaking my husband, Gus P'manolis, always generously provides me. He has fed me, counseled me, encouraged me not to whine, and joined me in driving all over the state these last few years as I researched and lectured on women writers in California's early state history. My children, Daniel and Rose, Heidi and Will, and my grandson, Jacob, all deserve my thanks for their patience with me.

And of course, I feel very grateful to Frances Fuller Victor, who will always remain in my memory as such a rich contributor to our Pacific Coast women's history and literature. Her courage, integrity, and insistence on truth impressed me more than I can say.

Ida Rae Egli

INTRODUCTION

When Frances Fuller Victor followed the sun west to California in 1863, she was filled with hope and enthusiasm. In front of her lay the Golden Gate and Walt Whitman's *New Empire,* a land he had described as "grander than before..." with a "new gender-neutral connotation to the term 'brotherhood.'" San Francisco was a city in the throes of a literary bonanza, making it possible for Victor to establish herself as one of California's leading writers.

For the next fourteen years, Victor worked as a journalist, historian, poet, and fiction writer. Then, in 1877, she published her finest personal statement, *The New Penelope and Other Stories,* a slim volume that included a novella, ten short stories, and forty poems. Unlike much of her more recent work, it was written for a popular rather than a scholarly audience; indeed, it was not only reviewed favorably, but quickly sold out its first printing. It has, ironically, outlasted her more "serious" writings, perhaps because, in this historical fiction, she brought her hopes and concerns for the West Coast women's movement together with her practical knowledge of the history of women during the gold rush period. Based in part on Homer's *The Odyssey,* "The New Penelope" takes the story of the long-patient Penelope, wife of the wandering Odysseus, and brings it into the social climate of the West during the nineteenth century. Perhaps, too, this work endures because Anna Greyfield, the "Penelope" of the Pacific Northwest, represents the thousands of women, not unlike Victor, who came West, not seeking gold, but a richer life.

Frances Fuller was born to Adonigh and Lucy Williams Fuller on May 23, 1826, in Rome, New York, the first of five daughters. Her father's ancestors were founders of Plymouth, Massachusetts; her mother's family could be traced back to Egbert, the first king of England. When she was four, her family moved to Erie, Pennsylvania, where she first attended school. At age nine, she was writing poems; by the time she was an adolescent, she was sending her poems to the local paper for publication. In 1839, her family moved once again, this time to Wooster, Ohio, where she marked the end of her formal schooling at the local girls' school. By this time, however, she knew how to educate herself; she was a reader with an affinity for history, popular culture, and classic literature, especially that of the ancient Greeks. Throughout her life, these Greek literary themes and allusions would surface in her writing.

When she was fourteen, the local paper published her first poem; she was so flattered that she wrote a new poem each week. Unsolicited, the publisher of the *Cleveland Herald* sent her fifteen dollars for one of her poems, and shortly thereafter, a different editor sent her five dollars for another. So, at a very young age, Frances Fuller determined that her life would be dedicated to writing.

In 1848, when Frances was twenty-two years old, a Boston house published her first novel, a rather prosaic romance, *Anizetta, the Gunjira, or, The Creole of Cuba*. It received mixed reviews. That same year, Frances and her sister, Metta Fuller, established formal connections with *The Home Journal,* a reliable family periodical, and together they published a successful book of poetry in 1851, earning them mention in *Female Poets of America*. Edgar Allen Poe, John Greenleaf Whittier, and others in literary circles encouraged Frances to continue writing. Over the next few years, she produced three dime novels and one of the Pocket Novels series; two others were published by the Beadle subsidiary in London as part of the American Library series. According to her biographer, Jim Martin, in *A Bit of a Blue: The Life and Work of Frances Fuller Victor*, "The stories gave fairly accurate portrayals of the struggles, hardships, and daily lives of the American pioneers."

Several major events influenced Frances's life about this time, when she was enjoying moderate success as a writer. In the spring of 1850, her father died. Frances was twenty-four. His death came just as she was about to embark for Europe with friends. She abandoned her plans and came home to help support her mother and siblings.

In 1853, she married Jackson Barritt. Two years later they set out to homestead a claim near Omaha, Nebraska. The young couple's farm property was close to the steadily-trodden route Mormons used between 1846 and 1847 on their way to Salt Lake City from Nauvoo, Illinois. Life on the prairie was hard, and Frances Fuller Barritt had little time or energy to write. She used her experience from these difficult, laborious years later, however, in her stories about the Pacific Northwest. By 1859 her marriage had failed, and Frances had moved back to New York City. She was divorced in 1862, at which time she was given back her maiden name.

In 1863, Frances Fuller married Henry Clay Victor, a naval engineer. In March of 1863, the couple left New York for San Francisco on the steamer *America*. Once across the Isthmus, she and Henry had a layover in Acapulco for twelve days. For Frances, these were blissful days; she was in her prime, petite but also powerful, intelligent, and in love. Socially, she could be shy; intellectually she rarely was. Throughout her life she "valued the truth above all else" and had "a restless yearning for something better." And she had found a kindred spirit in Henry: both were artists (he was a sketch master and painter), both loved to wander, and both were fiercely independent.

The gold rush of 1848, and the economic boom that followed in the 1850s and 1860s, brought together the necessary ingredients for a literature more closely responsive to California's early statehood years and idiosyncratic lifestyle than any written for another century. This literary bonanza was the natural result of California's unique, rowdy development as a frontier.

Most frontiers offer heightened opportunity for women and others of minority status, but the California frontier went several steps further. Money from the gold rush stimulated immediate development throughout the state. It spawned the boisterous city of San Francisco, which had a ratio of twelve men to one women in 1852, and no law except by vigilante committee. By 1860, San Francisco had drawn more college graduates per capita than any other city in the union; most of the easy gold had been mined, and the ratio of men to women had shifted to four to one. Theoretically, San Francisco should have assumed a quieter, more genteel existence. But as Franklin Walker in *San Francisco's Literary Frontier* points out, "Most frontiers insisted on settling down; this one refused to."

The San Francisco of 1863 in which Frances Fuller Victor arrived was perhaps the best place in the world for a writer, especially a woman writer. The frontier openness, wealth, risk, and the rambunctiousness of the gold rush era had created a free-thinking society where the unconventional was acceptable.

Culturally diverse with gold rush immigrants and geographically separated from "the states," California had developed a *laissez faire* quality. Women rejoiced in the new freedoms California offered. Some managed boardinghouses; a few even drove stagecoaches or mined gold. Educated women like Victor could write for one of the city's 132 periodicals or twenty-odd newspapers.

Even though the plum writing assignments and publishing invitations were offered mostly to men, San Francisco's women enjoyed a unique role. Talented local writers rose to the top, and they were allowed great latitude. As Gerald Haslam wrote, "[The] artists of the time reflected a distinctness still associated with the region; they believed themselves to be liberated from the East and from the Puritan past." Furthermore, the women's suffrage movement, and the accompanying social reforms, created an interest in gender issues, opening the door for women like Victor to write newspaper columns from a distinctively female perspective.

By the time Frances and Henry Victor had secured an apartment in the hub of the downtown and unpacked their bags, they were already smitten by San Francisco. Henry and other naval officers assigned to the *U.S.S. Narragansett* were to protect San Francisco Bay against possible raids by Confederate ships. While Henry was at sea, Frances, thirty-six, and by now a competent writer, wrote a weekly column about San Francisco for the *Evening Bulletin*. She received a higher salary than she had ever known. Soon she was also writing articles for the *Golden Era*. Her weekly columns were informational, often funny and saucy. She reported on political and social events, news, and issues that concerned women. She also addressed the less aesthetic side of San Francisco life: the bodies that floated on the surface of the bay, the ramshackle houses close to the wharf, the children running in the streets, and the prostitutes parading their goods near "Frenchtown."

In 1863, Victor assumed the *nom de plume* Florence Fane as byline for her *Evening Bulletin* columns. As Florence Fane, Victor quickly found a growing audience and became a well-known writer in San Francisco and the surrounding areas. In print, she sparred with the city's other noted journalists, among them Charles H.

Webb, a man of quick wit and impressive social ties. She recalled later that she and Webb "raced for precedence in the public favor with the result that most people said the two were one—for as usual, they decided that no woman could be as 'smart' as a man who was an acknowledged wit."

Her readers responded with candor to her columns, especially when she wrote on the status of women. At times, she used satire to make her point, such as when she poked fun at current attitudes through her description of ancient Roman mythology, which characterized women as animals. Other times, she took issues head-on, dispelling the notion that women make poor public speakers with her enthusiastic review of a lecture given by a female speaker.

One column, generated by a trip to the Comstock mines, might have been the impetus for "The New Penelope." Interviewing miners about their gold rush experiences, she was impressed by their spirit of adventure and the stories of the women they brought with them. Certainly these visits to the mines, besides creating nostalgic copy for her columns, gave her the idea and the material for "How Jack Hastings Sold His Mine." Once the miners knew she was Florence Fane, they heaped praise and mining stocks on her. These stocks might have eased the financial woes of her last years had she paid the assessments on them; in 1863, however, she felt immune to death or poverty.

In 1864, just over a year after her arrival in San Francisco, Frances was offered the position of editor at a newspaper called *New Era*. For a woman to be offered an editorship, even in liberal San Francisco, was remarkable. Frances had reached a comfortable plateau in her career, so it must have given her more than a moment's pause when Henry wrote, asking her to move with him to Portland. At the end of November 1864, Frances said good-bye to San Francisco and her *New Era* readers:

Dear ERA, mine is the same California story—I came, I saw, I went away again. To make the analogy complete, I shall have to return here once more, hungering and thirsting for the brightness of California skies, languishing for the tonic of San Franciscan airs...and years from now, when I am world-weary, sad and old, I shall return.

Arriving in Portland at five a.m. on December 26, 1864, in a sheeting downpour, she wondered if the storm was to be her prophecy. But by the beginning of January 1865, she and Henry were set up in Portland. Shortly thereafter, she was introduced to Addison Gibbs, owner of Oregon Iron Works and also governor of Oregon. When she mentioned to Gibbs that she was going to "study up" on the country she had come to make her home, perhaps create something that might show the rest of the world what Oregon was like, he suggested that the state legislature might pay her for writing a historical travelogue. This off-hand promise launched her into a thirty-year career as Oregon historian.

Off and on, for the next twenty years, Frances traversed her new state, as well as Washington, Idaho, and California, gathering material for books, while Henry, now resigned from the Navy, searched out other professions. She was searching for the "truth" that lay hidden in pioneer recollections, state legislative documents, and military records from the Pacific Coast states. Because she was attempting to do work traditionally reserved for men, she deliberately made contacts with prominent men who could provide her with access to resources. She was granted the patronage of Matthew Paul Deady, U.S. District Court judge, who had the most impressive historical library in Oregon. She also made the acquaintance of Jesse Applegate, an early settler in Oregon, known and admired around the state as the "Sage of Yoncalla," and interviewed him in 1865 for her book.

In that same year, through Judge Deady, she met Joe Meek, a frontiersman and naturalist who came to Oregon Territory with a company of fur trappers even before homesteading began. Meek became the folk-hero protagonist for her book about Oregon settlement, *The River of the West*, published in 1870. Although the book received enthusiastic reviews, Victor was criticized for not echoing the more popular version of the massacre of missionaries Marcus and Narcissa Whitman and their party at Waiilapu, near Walla Walla, Washington. Her research, however, would not allow her to deny her critical conclusion.

This stubborn faithfulness to objectivity eventually lead to her title as the "Mother of Oregon History." A major factor in Victor's literary success was her distrust of "remembered history." She had heard enough fictionalizing of actual events in interviews to convince her that human recollection was susceptible to romantic retelling. She certainly knew the difference between legend and history. Years later, in writing to Professor Frederic George Young of the University of Oregon, she cautioned:

> There should be always contemporaneous recorded history. It is my experience that little value attaches to any other evidence, and that confusion results from admitting hearsay testimony. My whole effort has been to weed out worthless authorities and to stamp out prejudices.

For thirty years she sought out history, often working as a nomadic investigative journalist, exploring the country alone, and writing by candlelight. In time, she grew to understand the original history of the Pacific Northwest as well as any person of her time. Between 1870 and 1900, she wrote eleven books, bringing to each the truth as she found it. Her fiction and poetry, especially "The New Penelope," were based on accurate histories and on her informed impressions of the characters who populated the West.

Throughout this period, Frances Fuller Victor also wrote frequently on the subject of women's suffrage. Her opinion was neither conservative nor liberal but somewhere in between. Before she could recommend the vote and equality for women, she felt that women had to earn the right, that voting was a privilege. She said that women had to learn to support one another, had to educate themselves to vote responsibly, and had to educate their children equally, despite gender. The major recipients of her reproofs were men who endorsed patriarchal systems. In an 1874 essay on women, she wrote:

> Mind is the same, whether it resides in a man's form or a woman's. All the laws of the mind, the soul, the affections, are the same in men and women, so far as observation or science can determine.

In the fall of 1874, as another wet Portland winter approached, Frances Fuller Victor boarded the steamer Ajax for San Francisco, where she hoped to find more work and better pay for her writing career. Also, as she knew from her previous residency, San Francisco offered "a chemistry; a tolerance of ideas, people, and lifestyles" that she felt would be more congenial to someone whose outlook on life was becoming less and less mainstream.

She once again found her saucy, irreverent journalistic voice, writing for the *Morning Call* under her new *nom de plume*, Dorothy D. As before, Victor continued to address the role of women in society, now campaigning for lone women: "Something must be done for so many intelligent human beings barely able to obtain food and shelter for themselves." Despite a zeal for social justice, she had not lost her sense of humor and irreverence: one of her columns cautioned against the dangers of trash literature for youngsters, another spoofed the rewards and dangers of love letters.

A year later, in November 1875, Frances returned to Portland when she learned of her husband's death in a steamer disaster off the coast of Washington. Frances had lived separately from Henry since 1868. Although she wrote little about this, between the lines of her essays on the status and lives of women, one might infer her disappointment about the separation. Their financial difficulties may have served as catalyst for the couple's separation, but it appears that both Henry and Frances were driven individualists and artists, not especially keen on settling into an ordinary lifestyle or even a permanent location. Henry's death was both an emotional and financial calamity for Frances.

Writing once again became the focus of her life. It paid so little, however, that occasionally she sought other employment. By 1877, living "on little cash and much hope," Frances finished preparing *The New Penelope and Other Stories* for publication. The book was inspired by Frances's two passions, history and the advancement of women. It was a commercial success, selling out one thousand copies. Reviews were impressive, despite its overt feminism during this Victorian era. Personifying the lone woman in a pioneer western setting, Anna Greyfield became the voice of the suffering 1870s woman—as did Penelope in the classic myth.

In 1878, Hubert Howe Bancroft went to Portland in search of Frances Fuller Victor, whose histories of Oregon he had read and appreciated. Bancroft had come to California in 1853, at the age of twenty-one, to open a bookstore. He became a wealthy entrepreneur and, by 1869, had decided to produce a definitive series of histories of the Pacific Northwest and wanted to hire Victor as one of his chief writers of the Bancroft Histories. From that visit, their twelve-year—often stormy—professional relationship began.

For years prior, Victor had been gathering materials for her own definitive history of Oregon, but had been unable to secure funding for it. Thus, when Hubert Bancroft approached her, she felt she was facing a *fait accompli*. She had the materials, but Bancroft had the money and resources. As she wrote, "I felt a good deal cut up by having my field invaded by another, not so well prepared, but who had a plump exchequer and an army of assistants....It was useless to compete with such superior forces."

On October 20, 1878, Frances headed for San Francisco to work in the Market Street "history factory" that Bancroft had set up to complement his library and house his staff of writers and aides. The pay was low, less than $100 a month, and working conditions were grueling. Even though she had signed a contract relinquishing her rights to her work, it was only later that she realized Bancroft meant to give her no authorship credit either. She admitted that she had "become so immersed in her subject that she gave little thought to who would actually receive credit for [her work]." And, as she was all too aware, "the bread and butter argument for silence proved effective in all cases." These were tiring years, but she was content to be back in San Francisco. She loved the city's liberal population and balmy seasons; her health was good; her sister and niece lived nearby; and she was home again.

By the early 1880s, she had finished the Oregon volumes. Later, she produced much of the history for the California, Washington, Idaho, and Montana volumes and some on Wyoming, Nevada, and Utah, completing no fewer than four full volumes of histories for Bancroft and contributing to others. She also wrote extensively about the "Indian issue" throughout the Pacific Coast states. She interviewed pioneers who were a part of the settlement process, as well as native peoples who were on the other side of the great struggle over the land.

Her biographer, Jim Martin, noted that on several occasions during her twelve-year tenure with Bancroft, Frances objected to her employer's practices. For instance, needing cash, he rushed the Oregon volumes into publication, choosing expediency over accuracy. As works were published, Bancroft began to solicit sizable sums from notable pioneers and state aristocrats in return for including their biographies. Victor protested, at first privately and finally publicly in 1893, when the *Bancroft Histories* were displayed at the World's Colombian Exposition in Chicago. Victor was there with four of the volumes she had produced—her name attached to each—along with a page of explanation. Bancroft never conceded Victor's authorship, saying only that she had furnished "much valuable raw material in a crude form, which I put into suitable condition for publication." Not so easily dismissed, but still not bitter, Victor wrote:

> I can truthfully say that whatever knowledge of Oregon history Mr. Bancroft possesses, he obtained from me. I do not mention that fact as a conspicuous defect in his education, for there was not much known on the subject 25 years ago, and at best, not every one can be a historian, but because I am fond of my work and am grieved that through too much editing it has failed somewhat of my purpose in performing a long and serious labor.

In the end, she was fairly well satisfied with her Oregon histories and was glad to finally see them in print. In May 1889, when she was sixty-three, Frances resigned her position with Bancroft. She spent a few months with her niece in Santa Cruz before traveling back to Portland to work on a revision of *All Over Oregon and Washington*. Realizing a revision would not be enough, she embarked on an entirely new work, *Atlantis Arisen, or, Talks of a Tourist about Oregon and Washington*. The book came out in 1891 and was another success, although remuneration was slim. That same year, the Oregon State Legislature voted to hire Frances Fuller Victor to produce a historical volume on the early Indian wars in Oregon. The book was issued in 1894 to good reviews, although veterans were disappointed that she had not interviewed them nor listed the muster rolls for the wars, which would have needlessly doubled the size of the book. Nevertheless, the book was a huge success.

Introduction

In 1894, Victor took active part in the Woman's Congress in San Francisco; 1901 saw the publication of a collection of forty years of poetry, simply titled, *Poems*. In between these triumphs, she suffered illness and a deep, unrelenting fatigue, a result of years of difficult and stressful work. Medical bills began to drain her meager purse. Sometimes, friends and associates helped her out financially. In desperation, she even concocted a plan to sell toiletries door-to-door. In November of 1899, she wrote to her longtime friend, Oliver Applegate:

> My health is still the same as you have seen it these last years, and never can be any better...But I keep on doing— that is the only way to enjoy life—is to use it. The end will come, of course, but it need not be met half way.

She died at three a.m. on the fourteenth of November, 1902, in a boarding-house room; only her proprietor, Emma Gilmore, was with her. Her grave in Portland's Riverview Cemetery was unmarked until October 1947, when it was dedicated by the Daughters of the American Revolution.

Although she possessed very little at the end of her life, Frances Fuller Victor left behind a wealth of written work. In particular, Victor's novella, "The New Penelope," and her short stories present valuable pictures of gold rush and West Coast life that are astonishingly accurate in detail. While the women who populate other stories of the gold rush—Bret Harte's, for example—often seem like simple literary devices, the women of Victor's works are wonderfully alive, sassy, troubled, conflicted, and intelligent. With the eyes of a historian, Victor places these characters in authentic settings and real-life struggles, giving her stories an enduring quality that makes them interesting and relevant more than one hundred years later.

For many years, readers have been content with the romantic and trite images of the gold rush: single-minded miners consumed with gold, straitlaced merchants trying to make a buck, prostitutes with hearts of gold, and dutiful wives tending to their children and homes. But the last several years have seen a broader interest in the gold rush experience, as scholars and the reading public have begun to wonder what really happened—what happened not only to white men, but also to women, the Chinese, the Indians, and the environment. The material in *Women of the Gold Rush* comes at an opportune time. Although they are clearly fiction, these stories give us unforgettable women characters who represent a range of experiences in the West. These stories enlarge our view of history and our understanding of women—as well as make for some lively and entertaining tales, both funny and suspenseful, with the power to capture, inform, and enthrall.

Like the characters she so carefully created, Frances Fuller Victor cannot be easily forgotten. For nearly forty years, she reveled in the landscape and life of the Pacific Northwest, authoring much of the original state histories that give each of us a sense of who we are and what we stand for. Emblematic of the indomitable West, she leaves us with her legacy of courage and integrity.

Ida Rae Egli
March 1998

THE NEW PENELOPE

I may as well avow myself in the beginning of my story as that anomalous creature—a woman who loves her own sex and naturally inclines to the study of their individual peculiarities and histories in order to get at their collective qualities. If I were to lay before the reader all the good and bad I know about them by actual discovery, and all the mean, and heroic, attributes this habit I have of studying people has revealed to me, I should meet with incredulity, perhaps with opprobrium. However that may be, I have derived great enjoyment from having been made the recipient of the confidences of many women, and by learning therefrom to respect the moral greatness that is so often coupled with delicate physical structure and almost perfect social helplessness. Pioneer life brings to light striking characteristics in a remarkable manner; because in the absence of conventionalities and in the presence of absolute and imminent necessities, all real qualities come to the surface as they never would have done under different circumstances. In the early life of the Greeks, Homer found his Penelope; in the pioneer days of the Pacific Coast, I discovered mine.

My wanderings, up and down among the majestic mountains and the sunny valleys of California and Oregon, had made me acquainted with many persons, some of whom were to me, from the interest they inspired me with, like the friends of my girlhood.

1

Among this select number was Mrs. Anna Greyfield, at whose home among the foothills of the Sierras in Northern California I had spent one of the most delightful summers of my life. Intellectual and intelligent without being learned or particularly bookish; quick in her perceptions and nearly faultless in her judgment of others; broadly charitable, not through any laxity of principle on her own part, but through knowledge of the stumbling blocks of which the world is full for the unwary, she was a constant surprise and pleasure to me. For among the vices of women I had long counted uncharitableness, and among their disadvantages want of actual knowledge of things—the latter accounting for the former.

I had several times heard it mentioned that Mrs. Greyfield had been twice married, and as her son Benton was also called Greyfield, I presumed that he was the son of the second marriage. How I found out differently I am about to relate.

One rainy winter evening, on the occasion of my second visit to this friend, we were sitting alone before a bright wood fire in an open fireplace when we chanced to refer to the subject of her son's personal qualities; he then being gone on a visit to San Francisco and of course very constantly in his mother's thoughts, as only sons are sure to be.

"Benton is just like his father," she said. "He is self-possessed and full of expedients, but he says very little. I have often wished he conversed more readily, for I admire a good talker."

"And yet did not marry one—the common lot!"

Mrs. Greyfield smiled and gazed into the fire, whose pleasant radiance filled the room, bringing out the soft warm colors in the carpet and making fantastic shadows of our easy chairs and ourselves upon the wall.

"Mr. Greyfield was your second husband?" I said, in an inquiring tone, but without expecting to be contradicted.

"Mr. Greyfield was my first, last, and only husband," she replied, with a touch of asperity, yet not as if she meant it for me.

"I beg your pardon," I hastened to explain, "but I had been told—"

"Yes, I can guess what you have been told. Very few people know the truth—but I never had a second husband, though I was twice married," and my hostess regarded me with a smile half-assumed and half-embarrassed.

For my own part, I was very much embarrassed, because I had certainly been informed that she had lived for a number of years with a second husband who had not used her well, and from whom she was finally divorced. Doubt her word I could not; neither could I reconcile her statement with facts apparently well-known. She saw my dilemma and, after a brief silence, mentally decided to help me out of it. I could see that in the gradual relaxing of certain muscles of her face, which had contracted at the first reference to this—as I could not doubt—painful subject. Straightening her fine form as if ease of position was not compatible with what was in her mind, she grasped the arms of her chair with either hand and, looking with a retrospective gaze into the fire, began:

"You see it was this way: the man I married the second time had another wife."

While she drew a deep breath and made a momentary pause, I seemed to take it all in, for I had heard so many stories of deserted Eastern homes and subsequent illegal marriages in California that I was prepared not to be at all surprised at what I should learn from her. Directly she went on:

"I found out about it the very day of the marriage. We were married in the morning, and in the afternoon a man came over from Vancouver who told me that Mr. Seabrook had a wife and family of children in a certain town in Ohio." Another pause followed, while she seemed to be recalling the very emotions of that time.

"Vancouver?" I said, "That is on the Columbia River."

"Yes, I was living in Portland at that time."

In reply to my glance of surprise, she changed the scene of her story to an earlier date.

"Mr. Greyfield had always wanted to come to California after the gold discoveries; but when he married me, he agreed not to think of it anymore. I was very young and timid, and very much attached to my childhood home and my parents; I could not bear the thought of going so long a distance away from them. It was not then, as it is now, an easy journey of one week, but a long six months' pilgrimage through a wilderness country infested by Indians. To reach what? Another wilderness infested by white barbarians!"

"But I have always heard," I said, "that women were idealized and idolized in those days."

"That is a very pretty fiction. If you had seen what I have seen on this coast, you would not think we had been much idealized. Women have a certain value among men when they can be useful to them. In the old States, where every man has a home, women have a fixed position and value in society, because they are necessary to make homes. But on this coast, in early times, and more or less even now, men found they could dispense with homes; they had been converted into nomads, to whom earth and sky, a blanket and a frying pan, were sufficient for their needs. Unless we came to them armed with endurance to battle with primeval nature, we became burdensome. Strong and coarse women who could wash shirts in any kind of a tub out-of-doors under a tree and iron them kneeling on the ground, to support themselves and half a dozen little, hungry, young ones, were welcome enough before the Chinamen displaced them. We had some value as cooks before men, with large means, turned their attention to supplying their brothers with prepared food for a consideration below what we could do with our limited means. And then the ladies, the educated, refined women, who followed their husbands to this country, or who came here hoping to share, perchance, in the golden spoils of the mines! Where are they today, and what is their condition? Look

for them in the sunless back rooms of San Francisco boardinghouses, and you will find them doing a little fine sewing for the
shops or working on their own garments, which they must make
out of school hours, because the niggardly pay of teachers in the
lower grades will not allow of their getting them done. Idealized
indeed! Men talk about our getting out of our places where we
clamor for paying work of some kind, for something to do that
will enable us to live in half-comfort by working more hours than
they do to earn lordly livings."

How muchsoever I might have liked to talk this labor question
over with my intelligent hostess at any other time, my curiosity
concerning her own history having been so strongly aroused, the
topic seemed less interesting than usual, and I seized the
opportunity given by an emphasized pause to bring her back to
the original subject.

"Did you come first to California?" I asked.

"No. I had been married a little over a year when Benton was
born. 'Now,' I thought, 'my husband will be contented to stay at
home.' He had been fretting about having promised not to take
me to California, but I hoped the baby would divert his thoughts.
We were doing well and had a pleasant house, with everything in
and about it that a young couple ought to desire. I deceived myself
in expecting Mr. Greyfield to give up anything he had strongly
desired, and seeing how much he brooded over it, I finally told
him to be comforted; that I would go with him to California if he
would wait until the baby was a year old before starting, and to
this he agreed."

"How old were you at that time?"

"Only about nineteen. I was twenty the spring we started, and
celebrated my anniversary by making a general gathering of all my
relatives and friends at our house before we broke up and sold off
our housekeeping goods—all but such as could be carried in our
wagons across the plains."

"You were not starting by yourselves?"

"O, no. There was a large company gathering together on the Missouri River to make the start in May, and we, with some of our neighbors, made ready to join them. I shall never forget my feelings as I stood in my own house for the last time, taking a lifelong leave of every familiar object! But you do not want to hear about that."

"I want to hear what you choose to tell me, but most of all about your second marriage, and what led to it."

"It is not easy to go back so many years and take up one thread in the skein of life and follow that alone. I will disentangle it as rapidly as I can; but first let us have a fresh fire."

Suiting the action to the word, my hostess touched a bell and ordered a good supply of wood, which I took as an intimation that we were to have one of our late sittings. In confirmation of this suspicion, a second order was given to have certain refreshments, including hot lemonade, made ready to await our pleasure. When we were once more alone, I begged her to go on with her story.

"We left the rendezvous in May and traveled without any unusual incidents all through the summer."

"I beg pardon for interrupting you, but I do want to know how you endured that sort of life. Was it not terrible?"

"It was monotonous, it was disagreeable, but it was not *terrible* while everybody was well. There were compensations in it, as in almost any kind of life. My husband was strong and cheerful, now that he was having his own way; the baby throve on fresh air and good milk—for we had milch cows with us—and the summer months on the grassy plains are delightful, except for rather frequent thunderstorms. The grass was good and our cattle in fine order. Everything was well until the cholera broke out among us."

"And then?"

"And then my husband died."

"Ah, what have not pioneer women endured!"

"Mr. Greyfield had from the first been regarded as a sort of leader. Without saying much, but by being always in the right place at the right time, he had gained an ascendancy over the less courageous, strong, and decided men. When the cholera came he was continually called upon to nurse the sick, to bury the dead, and to comfort the living."

"And so became the easier victim?"

My remark was unheeded while my hostess lived over again in recollection the fearful scenes of the cholera season on the plains. I wanted to divert her and called her attention to the roaring of the wind and beating of the rain without.

"Yes," she said, "it stormed just in that way the night before he died. We all were drenched to the skin, and he was not in a condition to bear the exposure. I was myself half-sick with fever, and when the shock came I became delirious. When I came to myself we were a hundred and fifty miles away from the place where he died."

"How dreadful!" I could not help exclaiming. "Not even to know how and where he was buried."

"Nor if he were buried at all. So frightened were the people in our train that they could not be prevailed upon to take proper care of the sick and dying, nor pay proper respect to the dead. After my reason returned, the one subject that I could not bear to have mentioned was that of my husband's death. Some of the men belonging to the train had taken charge of my affairs and furnished a driver for the wagon I was in. The women took care of Benton, and I lived, who would much rather have died. Probably I should have died, but for the need I felt, when I could think, of somebody to care for, support, and educate my child. My constitution was good, and that, with the anxiety about Benton, made it possible for me to live."

"My dear friend," I exclaimed, "what a dreadful experience! I wonder that you are alive and sit there talking to me, this moment."

"You will wonder more before I have done," she returned, with what might be termed a superior sort of smile at my inexperience.

"But how did you get to Oregon?" I asked, interrupting her again.

"Our train was about at the place where the Oregon and California emigrants parted company, when I recovered my reason and strength enough to have any concern about where I was going. Some of those who had started for Oregon had determined to go to California, and the most particular friend Mr. Greyfield had in the train had decided to go to Oregon instead of to California, as he first intended. Now, when my husband was hopeless of his own recovery, he had given me in charge of this man with instructions to be governed by him in all my business affairs, and I had no thought of resisting his will, though that bequest was the cause of the worst sorrows of my life, by compelling me to go to Oregon."

"Why cannot people be contented with ruling while living, without subjecting others to the domination of an irrevocable will, when they are no longer able to mold or govern circumstances? I beg your pardon. Pray go on. But first let me inquire whether the person to whom you were commanded to trust your affairs proved trustworthy?"

"As trustworthy as nearly absolute power on one side, and timid inexperience on the other, is likely to make anyone. When we arrived finally in Portland, he took my wagons and cattle off my hands and returned me next to nothing for them. Yet, he was about like the average administrator; it did not make much difference, I suppose, whether this one man got my property, or a probate court."

"Poor child! I can see just how you were situated. Alone in a new country, with a baby on your hands, and without means to make a home for yourself. What *did* you do? Did you never think of going back to your parents?"

"How could I get back? The tide of travel was not in that direction. Besides, I had neither money nor a sufficient outfit. There was no communication by mail in those days oftener than once in three months. You might perish a thousand times before you could get assistance from the East. O, no! There was nothing to be done except to make the best of the situation."

"Certainly you had some friends among your fellow immigrants who interested themselves in your behalf to find you a home? Somebody besides your guardian already mentioned."

"The most of them were as badly off as myself. Many had lost near friends. I was not the only widow, but some women had lost their husbands who had several young children. They looked upon me as comparatively fortunate. Men had lost wives, and these were the most wretched of all, for a woman can contrive some way to take care of her children, where a man is perfectly helpless. Families finding no houses to go into by themselves were huddled together in any shelter that could be procured. The lines of partition in houses were often as imaginary as the parallels of latitude on the earth, or were defined by a window or a particular board in the wall. O, I couldn't live in that way. My object was to get a real home somewhere. As soon as I could, I rented a room in a house with a good family, for the sake of the protection they would be to me, and went to earn a living. Of course, people were forward enough with their suggestions."

"Of what, for instance?"

"Most persons—in fact, everybody that I talked with—said I should have to marry. But I could not think of it; the mention of it always made me sick that first winter. I was recovering strength and was young, so I thought I need not despair."

"Such a woman could not but have plenty of offers, in a new country especially, but I understand how you must have felt. You could not marry so soon after your husband's death, and it revolted you to be approached on the subject. A wife's love is not so easily transferred."

"You speak as anyone might think, not having been in my circumstances. But there was something more than that in the feeling I had. I could not realize the fact of Mr. Greyfield's death.

It was as if he had only fallen behind the train and might come up with us any day. I *waited* for him all that winter."

"How distressing!" I could not help saying. Mrs. Greyfield sat silent for some minutes, while the storm raged furiously without. She rested her cheek on her hand and gazed into the glowing embers, as if the past were all pictured there in living colors. For me to say, as I did, "how distressing," no doubt seemed to her the merest platitude. There are no conventional forms for the expression of the utmost grief or sympathy. Silence is most eloquent, but I could not keep silence. At last I asked, "What did you do to earn a living?"

"I learned to make men's clothes. There was a clothing store in the place that gave me employment. First I made vests, and then pants, and finally I got to be quite expert and could earn several dollars a day. But a dollar did not buy much in those times; oh, the crying spells that I had over my work before I had mastered it sufficiently to have confidence in myself. Sancho Panza blessed the man that invented sleep. I say, blessed be the woman that invented crying fits, for they save thousands and thousands of women from madness annually!"

This was a return to that sprightly manner of speech that was one of Mrs. Greyfield's peculiar attractions and which often cropped out in the least expected places. But though she smiled, it was easy to see that tears would not be far to seek. "And yet," I said, "it is a bad habit to cultivate—the habit of weeping. It wastes the blood at a fearful rate."

"Don't I know it? But it is safer than frenzy. Why I used—but I'll not tell you about that yet. I set out to explain to you my marriage with Mr. Seabrook. As I told you, everybody said I must marry, and the reasons they gave were that I must have somebody to support me, that it was not safe for me to live alone, that my son would need a man's restraining hand when he came to be a few years older, and that I, myself, was too young to live without love. Therefore, the only correct thing to do was to take a husband—a good one, if you could get him—a husband, anyway. As spring came round, and my mind regained something of its natural elasticity, and my personal appearance probably improved with returned health, the air seemed full of husbands. Everybody that had any business with me, if he happened not to have a wife, immediately proposed to take me in that relation. All the married men of my acquaintance jested with me on the subject, and their wives followed in the same silly iteration. I actually felt myself of some consequence, whether by nature or by accident, until it became irksome."

"How did all your suitors contrive to get time for courtship?" I laughingly inquired.

"O, time was the least of their requirements. You know, perhaps, that there was an Oregon law, or rather, a United States law, giving a mile square of land to a man and his wife: to each, half. Now some of the Oregonians made this "Donation Act" an excuse for going from door-to-door to beg a wife, as they pretended, in order to be able to take up a whole section, though when not one of them ever cultivated a quarter section or ever meant to."

"And they came to *you* in this way? What did they say? How did they act?"

"Why, they rode a spotted Cayuse up to the door with a great show of hurry, jangling their Mexican spurs and making as much noise as possible. As there were no sidewalks in Portland then, they could sit on their horses and open a door, or knock at one, if they had so much politeness. In either case, as soon as they saw a woman they asked if she were married, and if not, would she marry? There was no more ceremony about it."

"Did they ever really get wives in that way, or was it done in recklessness and sport? It seems incredible that any woman could accept such an offer as that."

"There were some matches made in that way; though, as you might conjecture, they were not of the kind made in heaven, and

11

most of them were afterwards dissolved by legislative action or decree of the courts."

"Truly you were right when you said women are not idealized in primitive conditions of society," I said, after the first mirthful impulse created by so comical a recital had passed. "But how was it, that with so much to disgust you with the very name of marriage, you finally did consent to take a husband? He, certainly, was not one of the kind that came riding up to doors, proposing on the instant?"

"No, he was not, but he might as well have been for any difference it made to me," said Mrs. Greyfield, with that bitterness in her tone that always came into it when she spoke of Seabrook. "You ask how was it that I at last consented to take a husband? Do you not know that such influences, as constantly surrounded me, are demoralizing as I said? You hear a thing talked of until you become accustomed to it. It is as Pope says: You 'first endure, then pity, then embrace.' I endured, felt contempt, and finally yielded to the pressure.

"Why, you have no idea, from what I have told you, of the reality. My house, as I have already mentioned, was one room in a tenement. It opened directly upon the street. In one corner was a bed. Opposite the door was a stove for cooking and warming the house. A table and two chairs besides my little sewing chair completed the furnishings of the apartment. The floor was bare except where I had put down an old coverlet for a rug before the bed. Here in this crowded place I cooked, ate, slept, worked, and received company and offers!

"Just as an example of the way in which some of my suitors broached the subject, I will describe a scene. Fancy me kneeling on the floor, stanching the blood from quite a serious cut on Benton's hand. The door opens behind me, and a man I never have seen before thrusts his head and half his body in at the opening. His salutation is 'Howdy!'—his first remark, 'I heern thar was a mighty purty widder livin' here, and I reckon my infurmation was correct. If you would like to marry, I'm agreeable.'"

"How did you receive this candidate? You have not told me what you replied on these occasions," I said, amused at this picture of pioneer life.

"I turned my head around far enough to get one look at his face, and asking him rather crossly if there were any more fools where he came from, went on bandaging Benton's hand."

The recollection of this absurd incident caused the narrator to laugh as she had not often laughed in my hearing.

"This may have been a second Werther," I remarked, "and surely no Charlotte could have been more unfeeling than you showed yourself. It could not be that a man coming in that way expected to get any other answer than the one you gave him?"

"I do not know, and I did not then care. One day a man, to whose motherless children I had been kind when opportunity offered, slouched into my room without the ceremony of knocking and dropping into a chair as if his knees failed him, began twirling his battered old hat in an embarrassed manner, and doing as so many of his predecessors had done—proposing offhand. He had a face like a terra-cotta image, a long lank figure, faded old clothes, and a whining voice.

"He told me that he had no 'woman' and that I had no 'man,' a condition that he evidently considered deplorable. He assured me that I suited him 'fustrate,' that his children 'sot gret store by me' and 'liked my victuals,' and that he thought a 'heap' of my little boy. He also impressed upon me that he had been 'considerin' the 'rangement of jinin' firms for some time. To close the business at once, he proposed that I should accept of him for my husband then and there."

"And pray, what did you say to *him?*"

"I told him that I did not know what use I had for him, unless I should put him behind the stove and break bark over his head."

13

This reply tickled my fancy so much that I laughed until I cried. I insisted on knowing what put it into her mind to say that.

"You see, we burned fir wood, the bark of which is better to make heat than the woody portion of the tree, but is never sawed or split, and has to be broken. I used to take up a big piece and bring it down with a blow over any sharp corner to knock it into smaller fragments, and something in the man's appearance, I suppose, suggested that he might be good for that, if for nothing else. I did not stop to frame my replies on any forms laid down in young ladies' manuals, but they seemed to be conclusive as a general thing."

"I should think so. Yet, there must have been some, more nearly your equals, attracted by your youth and beauty, loving you or capable of loving you, to whom you could not give such answers, by whom such answers would not be taken."

"As I look back upon it now, I cannot think of anyone I might have taken and did not that I regret. There were men of all classes nearly, but they were not desirable as I saw it then or as I see it now. It is true that I was young, and pretty, perhaps, and that women were in a minority. But then, too, the men who were floating about on the surface of pioneer society were not likely to be the kind of men that make true lovers and good husbands. Some of them have settled down into steady-going benedicts and have money and position. The worst effect of all this talk about marrying was that it prepared me to be persuaded against my inner consciousness into doing that which I ought not to have done. My truer judgment had become confused, my perceptions clouded, from being so often assailed by the united majority who could not bear to see the poor, little minority go unappropriated. But come, let us have our cakes and lemonade. You need something to sustain you while I complete the recital of my conquests."

I felt that she needed a brief interval in which to collect her thoughts and calm a growing nervousness that in spite of her efforts at pleasantry would assert itself in various little ways, evident enough to my observation. A saucepan of water was set upon the hot coals on the hearth, the lemons cut and squeezed into two elegant goblets, upon square lumps of sugar that eagerly took up the keen acid and grew yellow and spongy in consequence. A sociable little round table was rolled out of its seclusion in a corner and made to support a tray between us, whereon were such dainty cakes and confections as my hostess delighted in.

There was an air of substantial comfort in all the arrangements of my friend's house that made it a peculiarly pleasant one to visit. It lacked nothing to make it homelike, restful, attractive. The house itself was large and airy with charming views; the furniture sufficiently elegant without being too fine for use; flowers, birds, and all manner of *curios* abounded yet were never in the way, as they so often are in the houses of people who are fond of pretty and curious things but have no really refined taste to arrange them. Our little ten o'clock lunch was perfect in its appointments—a "thing of beauty," as it was, of palatableness and refreshment. So strongly was I impressed at the moment with this talent of Mrs. Greyfield's that I could not refrain from speaking of it, as we sat sipping hot and spicy lemonade from those exquisite cut-glass goblets of her choosing and tasting dainties served on the loveliest china.

"Yes, I suppose it is a gift of God, the same as a taste for the high arts is an endowment from the same source. Did it never strike you as being absurd that men should expect, and as far as they can, require all women to be good housekeepers? They might as well expect every mechanic to carve in wood or chisel marble into forms of life. But it is my one available talent and has stood me in good stead, though I have no doubt it was one chief cause of my trouble by attracting Mr. Seabrook."

"You must know," I said, "that I am tortured with curiosity to hear about that person. Will you not now begin?"

"Let me see—where did I leave off? I was telling you that although I had so many suitors of so many classes, and none of them desirable to my way of thinking, I was really gradually being influenced to marry. You must know that a woman so young and so alone in the world, and who had to labor for her bread and her child's bread, could not escape the solicitations of men who did not care to marry; it was this class who gave me more uneasiness than all the presuming ignorant ones, who would honor me by making me a wife. I know it is constantly asserted, by men themselves, that no woman is approached in that way who does not give some encouragement. But no statement could be more utterly false—unless they determine to construe ordinary politeness and friendliness into a covert advance. The cunning of the "father of lies" is brought to bear to entrap artless and inexperienced women into situations whence they are assured there is no escape without disgrace.

"During my first year of widowhood my feelings were several times outraged in this way, and at first I was so humiliated and had such a sense of guilt that it made me sick and unfit for my work. The guilty feeling came, I now know, from the consciousness I had of the popular opinion I have referred to that there must be something wrong in my deportment. But by calling to mind all the circumstances connected with these incidents and studying my own behavior and the feelings that impelled me, I taught myself at last not to care so very much about it after the first emotions of anger had passed away. Still I thought I could perceive that I was not quite the same person, you understand—the 'bloom' was being brushed away."

"What an outrage! What a shame that a woman in your situation could not be left to be herself with her own pure thoughts and tender sorrows! Was there no one to whom you could go for advice and sympathy—none among all those who came to the country with you who could have helped you?"

"The people who came out with me were mostly scattered through the farming country and would have been of very little use to me if they had not been. In fact, they would probably have been first to condemn me, being chiefly of an uneducated class and governed more by traditions than by the wisdom of experience. There were two or three families, whose acquaintance I had made after arriving in Portland, who were kindly disposed towards me and treated me with great neighborliness, especially the family that was in the same tenement with me. To them I sometimes mentioned my troubles, but while they were willing to do anything for me in the way of a common friendly service, like the loaning of an article of household convenience, or sitting with me when Benton was sick—as he very often was—they could not understand other needs or minister to the sickness of the mind. If I received any counsel, it was to the effect that a woman was in every way better off to be married. I used to wonder why God had not made us married, why he had given us our individual natures, since there was forever this necessity of being paired!"

"Yet you had loved your husband?"

"I had never ceased to love him—and that was just what these people could not understand. Death cut *them* loose from everything, and they were left with only strong desires and no sentiment to sanctify them. That I should love a dead husband, and turn with disgust from a living one, was inexplicable to them."

"My dear, I think I see the rock on which you wrecked your happiness." For the moment I had forgotten what she had told me in the beginning, that Seabrook had married her illegally, and was imagining her married to a living husband and loving only the memory of one dead. She saw my error and informed me by a look. Pushing away the intervening table with its diminished contents and renewing the fire, Mrs. Greyfield proceeded:

"It would take too long to go over the feelings of those times and assign their causes. You are a woman who can put yourself in my place to a great extent, though not wholly, for there are some things that cannot be imagined and only come by experience."

"Benton was two years and a half old, a very delicate child suffering nearly all the time with chills and fever. I had occasional attacks of illness from the malaria, always to be met with on the clearing up of lowlands near a river. Still I was able to sew enough to keep a shelter over our heads and bread in our mouths until I had been a year in Portland. But I could not get ahead in the least and was often very low-spirited. About this time I made the acquaintance of Mr. Seabrook. He was introduced to me by a mutual acquaintance, and having a little knowledge of medicine, gave me both advice and remedies for Benton. He used to come in quite often, and look after the child, and praise my housekeeping, which probably was somewhat better than that of the average pioneer of those days. He never paid me any silly compliments or disturbed my tranquillity with lovemaking of any sort. Just for that reason I began to like him. He was twelve or fifteen years older than myself, and more than ordinarily fine-looking and intelligent. You have no idea, because you have never been so placed, what a comfort it was to me to have such a friend."

"Yes, I think I know."

"One day he said to me, 'Mrs. Greyfield, this sitting and sewing all day is bad for your health. Now, I should think, being so good a housekeeper, you might do very well by taking a few boarders, and I believe you could stand that kind of labor better than sewing.' We had a little talk about it, and he proposed trying to find me a house suited to the purpose, to which I very readily consented, for though I was wholly inexperienced in any business, I thought it better to venture the experiment than to keep on as I was doing."

"How did you expect to get furniture? Pardon me, but you see I want to learn all about the details of so strange a life."

"I don't think I expected anything or thought of all the difficulties at once."

"Which was fortunate, because they would have discouraged you."

"It is hard to say what has or has not been for the best. But for that boardinghouse scheme, I do not believe I should have married the man I did.

"As I was saying, Mr. Seabrook never annoyed me with attentions. He came and talked to me in a friendly manner and with a superior air that disarmed apprehension on that score. Mrs.—, my neighbor in the next room, once hinted to me that his visits were indicative of his intentions, and thereby caused me a sleepless night. But as *he* never referred to the subject, and as I was now full of my new business project, the alarm subsided. A house was finally secured, or a part of a house, consisting of a kitchen, dining room, and bedroom on the first floor, and the same number of rooms above. I had a comfortable supply of bedding and table linen; the trouble was about cabinet furniture. But as most of my boarders were bachelors who quartered themselves where they could, I got along very well."

"You made a success of it, then?"

"I made a success. I threw all my energies into it and had all the boarders I could cook for."

"Mr. Seabrook boarded with you—I conjecture that."

"Yes, and he took a room at my house. At first I liked it well enough; I had so much confidence in him. But in a short time I thought I could perceive that my other boarders were disposed to think that we looked toward a nearer relationship in the future. Perhaps they were justified in thinking so, as they could only judge from appearances, and I had asked Mr. Seabrook to take the foot of the table and carve, because I had so much else to do that it was impossible for me to do that also. Gradually he assumed more the air of proprietor than of boarder, but as he was so much older and wiser, and had been of so much service to me, I readily pardoned what I looked upon as a matter of no great consequence.

"It proved to be, however, a matter of very great consequence. I had been established in the new house and business four or five weeks when one evening, Benton being unusually ill, I asked Mr. Seabrook's advice about him. My bedroom was upstairs, against the partition which separated my apartments from those occupied by a family of Germans. I chose that room for myself because it seemed less lonely and safer for me to be where I could hear the voice of the little German woman and she could hear mine. In the same manner my kitchen joined onto hers, and we could hear each other at our work. Benton, being too ill to be dressed, was lying on the bed in my room, and I asked Mr. Seabrook to go up and look at him. He examined him and told me what to do, in his usual decided and assured manner, and went back to the dining room, which was also my sitting room. As soon as Benton was quieted, so that I could leave him, I also returned to the lower part of the house to finish my evening tasks.

"There is such a feeling of hatred that arises in my heart when I recall that part of my history that it makes me fear my own wickedness! Do you think we can hate so much as to curse and blight our own natures?"

"Undoubtedly, but that would be a sort of frenzy and would finally end in madness. *You* do not feel in that way. It is the overmastering sense of wrong suffered, for which there can be no redress. Terrible as the feeling is, it must be free from the wickedness you impute to yourself. Your nature is sound and sweet at the core—I feel sure of that."

"Thank you. I have had many grave doubts about myself. But to go on. Contrary to his usual habit, Mr. Seabrook remained at the house that evening and in the dining room instead of his own room. I was so busy with my work and anxious about Benton that I did not give more than a passing thought to him. He, also, seemed much preoccupied.

"At last my work was done, and I took a light to go to my

room, telling Mr. Seabrook to put out the lights below stairs, as I should not be down again. 'Stop a moment,' said he. 'I have something to tell you that you ought to know.' He very politely placed a chair for me, which I took. His manners were faultless in the matter of etiquette—how very far a fine manner goes in our estimate of people! I had not the shadow of a suspicion of what was coming. 'Mrs. Greyfield,' he said, with great gravity, 'I fear I have unintentionally compromised you very seriously. In advising you to take this house and open it for boarders, I was governed entirely by what I conceived to be your best interests, but it seems that I erred in my judgment. You are very young—only twenty-three, I believe, and—I beg your pardon—too beautiful to pass unnoticed in a community like this. Your boarders, so far, are all gentlemen. Further, it has been noticed and commented upon that—really, I do not know how to express it—that *I* have seemed to take the place in your household that—pray, forgive me, Mrs. Greyfield—only a husband, in fact or in expectancy, could be expected or permitted to occupy. Do you see what I mean?'

"I sat stunned and speechless while he went on. 'I presume your good sense will direct you in this matter, and that you will grasp the right horn of the dilemma. If you would allow me to help you out of it, you would really promote my happiness. Dear Mrs. Greyfield, permit me to offer you the love and protection of a husband, and stop these gossips' mouths.'"

"You do not think he had premeditated this?" I asked.

"I did not take it in then, but afterwards I saw it plainly enough. He pressed me for an answer, all the time plausibly protesting that although he had hoped some time to win my love, he had not anticipated the necessity for urging his suit as a matter of ex-pediency. In vain I argued that if his presence in the house was an injury to me, he could leave it. It was too late, he said. I indignantly declared that it was not my fault that my boarders were all men. I was working for my living and would just as willingly have boarded any other creature if I could have got my money for it—a monkey or a sheep—it was all the same to me. He smiled superiorly on my fretfulness, and when I at last burst into a passion of tears, bade me good night with such an air of being extremely forbearing and judicious that I could not help regarding myself as a foolish and undisciplined child.

"That night I scarcely slept at all. Benton was feverish, and I half wild. All sorts of plans ran through my head, but turn the matter over any way I would, it amounted to the same thing. The money I must earn must come from men. Whether I sewed or cooked, or whatever I did, they were the paymasters to whom I looked for my wages. How, then, was it possible to escape contact with them or avoid being misunderstood? In one breath I resented, with all the ardor of my soul, the impertinence of the world's judgment, and in the next I declared to myself that I did not care, that conscious innocence should sustain me, and that I had a right to do the best I could for myself and child.

"But that was only sham courage. I was morally a coward and could not possibly face the evil spirit of detraction. Therefore, the morning found me feverish in body and faint in spirit. I kept out of sight of my boarders, except Mr. Seabrook, who looked into the kitchen with a sympathizing face, and inquired very kindly after Bennie, as he pet-named Benton. When my dinner was over that day, I asked the little German woman to keep the child until I could go on an errand and went over to Mrs.—, my old housemate, to get advice.

"Do you know how much advice is worth? If you like it, you haven't needed it; and if you do not like it, you will not take it. Mrs.— told me that if she were in my place—as if she *could* be in my place!—she would get rid of all her troubles by getting some man to take charge of her and her affairs. When I asked, with transparent duplicity, where I was to get a man for this service, she laughed in my face. People *did* talk so then, and what Seabrook said was the unexaggerated truth. It did not occur to me to examine into the authorship of the rumors; I was too shrinking and sensitive for that.

"When I reached home I found Mr. Seabrook at the house. A sudden feeling of anger flashed into my mind and must have illuminated my eyes, for he gave me one deprecating glance and immediately went out. This made me fear I was unjust to him. That evening he did not come to tea but sent me a note saying he had business at Vancouver and would not return for two or three days, but that when he did return it would be better to have my mind made up to dismiss him entirely out of the country or to have our engagement made known.

"That threw the whole responsibility upon me, and it was, as he knew it would be, too heavy for my twenty-three years to carry. To lose the most helpful and agreeable friend I had in the country, to banish him for no fault but being too kind to me, or to take him in place of one whose image would always stand between us—that was the alternative.

"The next day an incident occurred that decided my destiny. I had to go out to make some purchases for the house. At the store where I usually bought provisions, I chanced to meet a woman who had crossed the continent in my company, and she turned her back upon me without speaking. She was an ignorant, bigoted sort of woman of an uncertain temper, and at another time I might not have cared for the slight, but coming at a time when I was in a state of nervous alarm, it cut me to the quick. With great difficulty I restrained my tears and left the store. While hurrying home with a basket on my arm, almost choked with grief, I passed a kind, old gentleman who had always before had a pleasant word for me and an inquiry about my child. He, too, passed me with only the slightest sign of recognition. I thought my heart would burst in my breast, so terrible was the sense of outrage and shame—"

"Which was, after all, probably imaginary," I interrupted. "The insult of the ignorant ill-tempered woman was purely an accidental display of those qualities, and the slight recognition of your old friend the consequence of the other, for your face certainly expressed the state of your feelings, and your friend was surprised into silence by seeing you in such distress."

"That, very likely, is the true explanation. But it did not so impress me then. You cannot, in the state of mind I was in, go after people and ask them to tell you whether or not they really mean to insult you, because you are only too certain that they do. I was sick with pain and mortification. How I got through my day's work I do not remember, but you can understand that my demoralization was complete by this time, and that when Mr. Seabrook returned I was like wax in his hands. All that I stipulated for was a little more time; he had my permission to announce our engagement.

"My boarders and everyone who spoke to me about it congratulated me. When I look back upon it now, it seems strange that no one ever suggested to me the importance of knowing the antecedents of the man I was going to marry, but they did not. It seemed to be tacitly understood that antecedents were not to be dragged to light in this new world and that 'bygones should be bygones.' As to myself, it never occurred to my inexperience to suspect that a man might be dishonorable, even criminal, though he had the outside bearing of a gentleman."

"Did he propose to relieve you of the necessity of keeping boarders?"

"No. The business was a good one, and, as I have said, I was a success in this line. My constitution was good, my energy immense in labor, my training in household economy good, and, besides, I had a real talent for pleasing my boarders. I was to be provided with a servant, and the care of the marketing would devolve upon Mr. Seabrook. With this amelioration of my labors, the burden could be easily borne for the sake of the profits."

"What business was Mr. Seabrook in?"

"I never thought of the subject at that time. He was always well-dressed, associated with men of business who seemed to have money, and I never doubted that such a man was able to do anything he proposed. Women, you know, unconsciously attribute at least an earthly omnipotence to men. Afterwards, of course, I was disillusioned. But I must hasten, for it is growing late, and either the storm or these old memories shake my nerves.

"I had asked for a month's time to prepare my mind for my coming marriage. At the end of a week, however, Mr. Seabrook came to me and told me that imperative business called him away for an absence of several weeks, and that, in his judgment, the marriage ceremony should take place before he left. He should be away over the month I had stipulated for, and, in case of accident, I would have the protection of his name. My objections were soon overruled, and on the morning of his departure we were married— as I believed, legally and firmly bound—in the presence of my family of boarders and two or three women, including Mrs.—. He went away immediately, and I was left to my tumultuous thoughts."

"May I be permitted to know whether you loved him at all, at that time? It seems to me that you must have sometimes yearned for the ownership of some heart and the strong tenderness of man's firmer nature."

Mrs. Greyfield looked at me with a curiously mixed expression, half of sarcastic pity, half of amused contempt. But the thought, whatever it was, went unspoken. She reflected a moment silently before she answered.

"I have told you that my heart remained unweaned from the memory of my dead husband. I told Mr. Seabrook the same. But I admired, respected, and believed in him; he was agreeable to me and had my confidence. There can be no doubt, but if he had been all that he seemed, I should have ended by loving him in a quiet and constant way. As it was, the shock I felt at the discovery of his perfidy was terrible.

"My ears were yet tingling with my new name, when, everybody having gone, I sat down with Benton on my lap to have the pleasure of the few natural tears that women are bound to shed over their relinquished freedom. I was very soon aroused by a knock at the door, which opened to admit an old acquaintance, then residing in Vancouver, and a former suitor of mine.

"Almost the first thing he said was, 'I hear you have been getting married?'

"'Yes,' I said, trying to laugh off my embarrassment, 'I had to marry a man at last to get rid of them!'

"'You made a poor selection, then,' he returned, rather angrily.

"His anger roused mine, for his tone was, as I thought, insolent. 'Do you think I should have done better to have taken you?' I asked scornfully.

"'You would at least have got a man that the law could give you,' he retorted, 'and not another woman's husband.'

"The charge seemed so enormous that I laughed in his face, attributing his conduct to jealous annoyance at my marriage. But something in his manner, in spite of our mutual excitement, unsettled my confidence. He was not inventing this story; he evidently believed it himself. 'For God's sake,' I entreated, 'if you have any proof of what you say, give it to me at once!' And then he went on to tell me that on the occasion of Mr. Seabrook's late visit to Vancouver, he had been recognized by an emigrant out from Ohio, who met and talked with him at the Hudson's Bay store. That man had told him, my informant, that he was well-acquainted with the family of Mr. Seabrook, and that his wife and several children were living when he left Ohio.

"'Can you bring this man to me?' I asked, trembling with horrible apprehensions.

"'I don't know as I could,' said he, 'for he went, I think, over to the Sound to look up a place. But I can give you the name of the town he came from, if that would be of any use.' I had him write the address for me, as I was powerless to do it for myself.

"'I am sorry for you,' he said, as he handed me the slip of paper, 'that is, if you care anything for the rascal.'

"'Thank you,' I returned, 'but this thing is not proven yet. If you really mean well by me, keep what you have told me to yourself.'

"'You mean to live with him?' he asked.

"'I don't know what I shall do; I must have time to think.'

"'Very well, it is no affair of mine. I don't want a bullet through my head for interfering, but I thought it was no more than fair to let you know.'

"'I am very grateful, of course—I mean I am if there is any occasion, but this story is so strange and has come upon me so suddenly that I cannot take it all in at once with all its consequences.'

"'I know what you think,' he said finally. 'You suspect me of making up this thing to be revenged on you for preferring Seabrook to me. I'd be a damned mean cuss to do such a turn by any woman, wouldn't I? As to consequences, if the story is true, and I believe it is, why, your marriage amounts to nothing, and you are just as free as you were before!'

"I fancied his face brightened up with the idea of my freedom, and a doubt of his veracity intruded upon my growing conviction. Distracted, excited, pressed down with cares and fears, I still had to attend to my daily tasks. I begged him to go away and not to say a word to any other mortal about what he had told me, and he gave me the promise I desired. That was a fatal error, and fearfully was I punished."

"How an error? It seems to me quite remarkable prudence for one in your situation."

"So I thought then, but the event proved differently."

"Pray do tell me how you bore up under all this excitement and the care and labor of a boardinghouse? The more I know of your life, the more surprised I am at your endurance."

"It was the care and labor that saved me, perhaps. At all events, here I am, alive and well, tonight. I sometimes liken myself to a tree that I know of. It was a small fir tree in a friend's garden. For some reason it began to pine and dwindle and turn red. My friend's husband insisted on cutting it down, as unsightly, but this she objected to, until all the leaves were dry and faded and the tree apparently dead. Still she asked for it to be spared for another season, and, taking a stick, she beat the tree all over until not a leaf was left on a single bough, and there it stood, a mere frame of dry branches until everybody wished it out of the way. But behold! At last it was covered with little green dots of leaves that rapidly grew to the usual size, and now that tree is the thriftiest in my friend's garden and living evidence of the uses of adversity. But for the beating it got, it would now be a dead tree! I had my child to live and work for, and really, but for this last trouble, I should have thought myself doing well. I had found out how I could make and lay up money and was gaining that sense of independence such knowledge gives. Besides, I was young, and in good physical health most of the time before this last and worst stroke of fortune. *That* broke down my powers of resistance in some directions, I had so much to resist in others."

"Do you see what o'clock it is?" I asked.

"Yes, but if you do not mind sitting up, let's make a night of it. I feel as if I could not sleep—as if something were going to happen."

Very cheerfully I consented to the proposed vigil. I wanted to hear the rest of the story, and I knew she had a sort of prophetic consciousness of coming events. If she said "something was going to happen," something surely did happen. So the fire was renewed, and we settled ourselves again for "a night of it."

"What did you do, and why do you say that you committed a fatal error by keeping silence?"

"By suffering the matter to rest, I unfortunately fixed myself in the situation I would have avoided. My object was what yours would have been, or any woman's—to save all scandal until the facts were known to a certainty. I was so sensitive about being talked over, and besides, felt that I had no right to expose Mr. Seabrook to a slanderous accusation. It was not possible for me to have foreseen what actually happened.

"I took one night to think the matter over. It was a longer night than this one will seem to you. My decision was to write to the postmaster of the town from which Mr. Seabrook was said to come. *Now* that would be a simple affair enough; the telegraph would procure us the information wanted in a day. *Then* a letter was five or six months going and coming. In the meantime, I had resolved not to live with Mr. Seabrook as his wife, but you will see how I would, under the circumstances, be compelled to seem to do so. I did not think of that at first, however. You know how you mentally go over impending scenes beforehand? I meant to surprise him into a confession, if he were guilty, and believed I should be able to judge of his innocence, if he should be wrongly accused. I wrote and dispatched my letter at once, and under an assumed name, to prevent its being stolen. When that was done I tried to rest unconcerned, but, of course, that was impossible. My mind ran on this subject day and night.

"The difficulties of my position could never be imagined; you would have to be in the same place to see them. Everybody now called me Mrs. Seabrook, and I could not repudiate the name without sufficient cause. I was forced to appear to have confidence in the man I had married of my own free will. Besides, I really did not know, of a verity, that he was not worthy of confidence. It seemed quite as credible that another man should invent a lie as that Mr. Seabrook should be guilty of an enormous crime.

"Naturally, I had a buoyant temper, was inclined to see the amusing side of things, enjoyed frolicsome conversations, and, in a general way, was well-fitted to bear up under worries and recover quickly from depressed conditions. The gentlemen who boarded with me were a cheerful and intelligent set, whose conversation entertained me, as they met three times a day at the table. They were all friends of Mr. Seabrook, which gave them the privilege of saying playful things to me about him daily. To these remarks I must make equally playful replies or seem ungracious to them. You will see how every such circumstance complicated my difficulties afterwards.

"You know, too, how pliable we all are at twenty-three—how often our opinions waver and our emotions change. I was particularly mercurial in my temperament before the events I am relating hardened me. I often laid in a half-waking state almost all night, my imagination full of horrible images, and when breakfast-time came, and I listened to an hour of entertaining talk, with frequent respectful allusions to Mr. Seabrook and kindly compliments to myself, these ugly visions took flight while I persuaded myself that everything would come out right in the end.

"A little while ago you asked me if I did not love Mr. Seabrook at all—did not long for tenderness from him? The question roused something of the wickedness in me that I confessed to you before, but I will answer the inquiry now by asking *you* if you think any woman in her twenties is quite reconciled to live unloved? I had not wished to marry again, yet undoubtedly there was a great blank in my life, which my peculiarly friendless condition made me very sensible of, and there was a yearning desire in my heart to be petted and cared for, as in my brief married life I had been. But the coarseness and intrusiveness I had experienced in my widowhood had made me as irritable as the 'fretful porcupine' towards that class of men. The thought of Mr. Seabrook loving me had never taken root in my mind. Even when he proposed marriage, it had seemed much more a matter of expediency than of love. But when, after I had accepted him as an avowed lover, his conduct had continued to be unintrusive and delicately flattering to my womanly pride, it was most natural that I should begin to congratulate myself on the prospect before me of lifelong protection from such wounds as I had received, with the great satisfaction of increased dignity in point of social position, for then, much more than now, and in a new country more than in an old one, a woman's position depended on her relationship to men; the wife of the most worthless man being the superior of an unmarried woman. Accordingly, I felt my promised importance and began to exult in it."

"In short, you were preparing to become much more subject to the second love than the first; a not infrequent experience," I interrupted. "You certainly must have loved a handsome, agreeable, courteous, and manly man, who would have interposed between you and the rude shocks of the world, and you had begun to realize that you could, in spite of your first love?"

"And to have a feeling of disappointment when the possibility presented itself that after all these blessings might be wrested from me, and of horror when I reflected that in that case my last estate would be inexpressibly worse than the first."

"There was a terrible temptation there!"

"No, that was the one thing I was perfectly clear about. Not to be dragged into crime or deserved disgrace, I was determined upon. How I should avoid it was where I was in doubt."

"I am very anxious to know how you met him on his return."

"There was no one in the house except myself and Benton, who was now quite well again for the time. I was standing by the dining room window, arranging some ferns in a hanging basket, and Benton was amusing himself with toys the boarders were always giving him. I heard a footstep and turned my head slightly to see who it was. Mr. Seabrook stood in the door, regarding us with a pleased smile.

"'How are my wife and boy?' he said cheerily, advancing towards me and proffering a kiss of greeting.

"I put up my hand to ward him off, and my heart stood motionless. I seemed to be struck with a chill. My teeth chattered together, while the ends of my fingers turned cold at once.

"Naturally, he was surprised, but thinking perhaps that the suddenness of his return, under the circumstances, had overcome me, he quickly recovered his tenderness of manner.

"'Have I frightened you, my darling?' he asked, putting out his arms to fold me to his breast. Not being able to speak, I whirled round rapidly and hastened to place the table between us. Of course, he could not comprehend such conduct but thought it some nervous freak, probably.

"Turning to Benton, he took him up in his arms and kissed him, asking him some questions about himself and toys. 'Could you tell me what is the matter with your mamma, Bennie?' he asked, seeing that my manner remained inexplicable.

"'I tink see has a till,' answered Benton, who by this time knew the meaning of the word 'chill' by experience.

'She has given *me* one, I know,' said Mr. Seabrook, regarding me curiously. I began to feel faint and sat down, leaning my head on my hand, my elbow on the table.

"'Anna,' said he, addressing me by my Christian name for the first time and giving me a little shock in consequence—for I had almost forgotten I had ever been called 'Anna'—'if I am so disagreeable to you, I will go away again, though I certainly had reason to expect a different reception.'

"'No,' I said, suddenly rousing up, 'you must not go until I have told you something, unless you go to stay—which would perhaps be best.'

"'To stay! Go to stay? There seems great need of explanation here. Will you be good enough to tell me why I am to go away to stay?'

"'The reason is, Mr. Seabrook,' I answered, 'that your true wife and your own children expect you at home, in Ohio.'

"I had worded my answer with the intention of shocking the truth out of him, if possible. If he should be innocent, I thought, he would forgive me. There was too much at stake to stand upon niceties of speech, and I watched him narrowly."

"How did he receive such a blow as that? I am curious to know how guilty people act, on being accused."

"You cannot tell an innocent from a guilty person," Mrs. Greyfield returned, with a touch of that asperity that was sometimes noticeable in her utterances. Then, more quietly: "Both are shocked alike at being accused; one because he is innocent, the other because he is guilty. How much a person is shocked depends upon temperament and circumstance. The guilty person, always consciously in danger of being accused, is likely to be prepared and on the defensive, while the other is not.

"What Mr. Seabrook did was to turn upon me a look of keen observation, not unmixed with surprise. It might mean one thing, it might mean another; how could I tell? He always impressed me so with his superiority that even in that moment when my honor and life's happiness were at stake, I was conscious of a feeling of abasement and guiltiness that I dare accuse *him* to his face. Perhaps he saw that I was frightened at my own temerity; at all events he was not thrown off his guard.

"'Do I understand you to charge me with crime—a very ugly crime, indeed?' he asked pointedly.

"'You know,' I said, 'whether you are guilty. If you are, may God so deal with you as you have meant to deal with me.'

"I fancied that he winced slightly at this, but in my excitement could not have seen very clearly. He knitted his brows and took several turns up and down the room.

"'If I knew who had put this monstrous idea into your mind,' he finally said with vehemence, 'I would send a bullet through his heart!'

"'In that case,' I replied, 'you could not expect me to tell you,' and I afterwards made that threat my excuse for concealing the name of my informant.

"Mr. Seabrook continued to pace the floor in an excited manner, stroking his long blonde beard rapidly and unconsciously. I still sat by the table, trying to appear the calm observer that I was not. He came and stood by me, saying, 'Do you believe this thing against me?'

"'I do not know what to believe, Mr. Seabrook,' I replied, 'but something will have to be done about this rumor.' I could not bear to go on, but he understood me. He leaned over my chair and touched my cheek with his.

"'Are you my wife or not?' he asked. I shuddered and put my face down on my hands. He knelt by my side and, taking my hands in his, so that my face must be seen, asked me to look into his eyes and listen to him. What he said was this:

"'If I swear to you, by Almighty God, that you are my true and only wife, will you then believe me?'"

Mrs. Greyfield was becoming visibly agitated by these reminiscences and paused to collect herself.

"You dared not say 'yes,'" I cried, carried away with sympathy, "and yet, you could not say 'no.' What did you do?"

"I burst into a passion of tears and cried convulsively. He would have caressed and consoled me, but I would have none of it.

"'Anna, what a strange homecoming for a bridegroom!' he said reproachfully.

"'Go away and leave me to myself,' I entreated. 'You must not stay here.'

"'What madness!' he exclaimed. 'Do you wish to set everybody to talking about us?' Ah! 'Talking about us' was the bugbear I most dreaded, and he knew it. But I wanted to seem brave, so I said that in private matters we were at liberty to do as we thought right and best.

"'And I think it right and best to stay where my wife is. Anna, what is to be the result of this strange suspicion of yours but to make us both unhappy and me desperate! Why, I shall be the laughingstock of the town—and I confess it is more than I can bear without flinching, to have it circulated about that Seabrook married a wife who cut him adrift the first thing she did. And then look at your position, too, which would be open to every unkind remark. You must not incur this almost certain ruin.'

"'Mr. Seabrook,' I said, more calmly than I had yet spoken, 'what you have said has suggested itself to me before. Stay here, then, if you must, until I can take measures to satisfy myself of the legality of our marriage. You can keep your own counsel, and I can keep mine. I have spoken to no one about this matter, nor will I for the present. There is your old room, your old place at the table. I will try to act as natural as possible; more than this you must not expect of me.' This businesslike tone nettled him.

"'May I inquire, Mrs. Seabrook, how long a probation I may anticipate, and what measures you intend taking to establish my good or bad character? A man may not be willing to wait always for a wife.'

"'Very well,' I replied to this covert threat, 'when you tire of waiting, you know what to do.' But my voice must have trembled, for he instantly changed his manner. There was more chance of winning me through my weakness than of intimidating me, coward though I was.

"'My dear Anna,' he said kindly, 'this is a most mortifying and trying predicament that I am in, and you must pardon me if I seem selfish. I do not know how I am to bear several months of this unnatural life you propose, and in thinking of myself I forget you. Yet your case, as *you* see it, is harder than mine, and I ought to pity and comfort you. If my darling would only let me!' He stretched out his arms to me. It was all I could do to keep from

35

rushing into them and sobbing on his breast. I was so tempest-tossed and weary—what would I not have given to lay down my burdens?"

"That is where the unrecognized heroism of women comes in. How few men would suffer in this way for the right! Had you chosen to ignore the tale that you had heard and taken this man who fortune had thrown with you upon this far-off coast, he might have been to you a kind friend and protector. Do you not think so?"

"Very likely. Plenty of bad men, when deferred to, have made good husbands, as men go. But I, by resisting the will of one bad man, made infinite trouble for myself. Are you becoming wearied?"

"No, no, go on."

"I must pass over a great deal, and, thank God! Some things have been forgotten. Mr. Seabrook took his old room downstairs. As before, he sat at the foot of the table and carved, but now as master of the house. Servants not being easily obtained, it was not remarked that my duties prevented my sitting down with my supposed husband at meals. He marketed for me and received the money of my boarders when payday came, and at first he did— what he failed to do afterwards—pay the money over to me.

"You are curious to know how Mr. Seabrook conducted himself toward me personally and in particular. For a few days, well; so that I began to feel confidence that so honorable a gentleman would be proved free from all stain. But he soon began to annoy me with the most persistent courtship, looking, as I could see, to breaking down my reserve, and subjecting me to the domination of a passion for him. If I had ever really loved Mr. Seabrook, it would have been a love of the senses, of interest, of the understanding, and not of the imagination and heart. I was just on the eve of such a love when it was fortunately put in check by my suspicions. For him to endeavor to create a feeling now that might, nay, that was intended to subvert principle and virtue, appeared even to my small worldly sense, an insult and an outrage.

"When I talked in this way to him, he half-laughingly and half in earnest always declared that I should get into the habit of forgetting our marriage before my 'proofs' came from Ohio—unless he every day put me in mind of it!—and this willingness to refer to 'proofs' threw me off my guard a little. He designed very cunningly, but not quite cunningly enough. As time wore on, and he feared the proofs might come before he had bent me to his will, his attempts lost even the semblance of love or decency. Many and many a night I feared to close my eyes in sleep, lest he should carry out his avowed purpose, for locks and bolts in a house in those days were considered unnecessary, and I improvised such defenses as I could. I used to threaten to call in my little German neighbor, to which he replied, 'she would probably recognize a man's right to occupy the same apartment with his wife!' Still, I think he was deterred somewhat by the fear of exposure from using violence."

The recital of such sufferings and anxieties as these, endured, too, by a young and lonely woman, affected me powerfully. My excited imagination was engaged in comparing the Mrs. Greyfield I saw before me—wearing her nearly fifty years with dignity and grace, full of a calm and ripe experience, still possessing a dark and striking beauty—with the picture she had given me of herself at twenty-three. What a wonder it was that with her lively temperament either for pain or pleasure, with her beauty and her helplessness, she had come out of the furnace unscathed, as she now appeared.

"How could you," I said, with a feeling of deep disgust, "how *could* you allow such a man to remain in your house?"

"How could I get him out? We were legally married so far as anybody in Oregon knew, except himself. Everybody presumed us to be living amicably together. He was careful to act the courteous gentleman to me in the presence of others. If we never went out together, it was easily explained by reference to my numerous household cares and Benton's frequent illness. As I before said, no one could understand the position who had not been in it. I could not send him away from me, nor could I go away from him. He would have followed me, he said, to the 'ends of the earth.' Besides, where could I go? There was nothing for me but to endure until the answer to my letter came. Never was a letter so anxiously desired as that one, for, of course, I fully expected that whatever news it contained would bring relief in some way. But I had made up my mind to his guilt, rightly judging that, had he been innocent, he would either have found means to satisfy me or have gone away and left me altogether.

"It had been six or seven months since my marriage. I had a large family of boarders to cook for, and Benton giving me a great deal of worry, fearing I should lose him. Working hard all day and sleeping very little nights, with constant excitement and dread, had very much impaired my health. My boarders often said to me: 'Mrs. Seabrook, you are working too hard; you must make Mr. Seabrook get you a cook.' What could I say in return, except to force a smile, and turn the drift of the conversation? Once, carried away with indignation, I replied that 'Mr. Seabrook found it as much as *he* could do to collect the money I earned!'"

"And you were set down at once as a vixen!" I said, smiling.

"Well, they were not expected to know how matters stood, when I had taken so much pain to conceal the truth. I was sorry I had not held my peace a little longer or altogether. Men never can understand a woman's right to resent selfishness, however atrocious, even when they are knowing to it, which in this case they were not. I might as well have held my tongue, since every unguarded speech of mine militated against me afterwards."

"You allowed Mr. Seabrook to have all your earnings?"

"I could not prevent it; he was *my husband*. Sometimes I thought he meant to save up all he could, to take him out of the country when the hoped-for proofs of his crime should arrive. And in that light I was inclined to rejoice in his avarice. I would have given all

I had for that purpose. O, those dreadful, dreadful days! When I was so near insane with sleeplessness and anxiety that I seemed to be walking on the air! Such, indeed, was my mental and physical condition that everything seemed unreal, even myself, and it surprises me now that my reason did not give way."

"Did you never pray?"

"My training had been religious, and I had always prayed. This, I felt, entitled me to help, and yet help did not come. I felt forsaken of God, and sullenly shut my lips to prayer or complaint. All severely tried souls go through a similar experience. Christ himself cried out, 'My God, my God, why hast thou *forsaken* me!'"

"No wonder you felt forsaken, indeed."

"You think I was as tried as I could be then, when I had a hope of escape, but worse came after that—worse, because more hopeless."

"You were really married to him then?" I cried in alarm. "I thought you told me in the beginning that you were not."

"Neither was I, but that did not release me. When at last I received an answer to my inquiries, confirming the statement of the immigrant from Ohio, it was too late."

"You do not mean—" I interrupted, in a frightened voice.

"No, no! I only mean that I had committed a great error in keeping silence on the subject at the first. You can imagine one of your acquaintances who had been several months peaceably living with a man of good appearance and repute, to whom you had seen her married, suddenly declaring her husband a bigamist and refusing to live with him, and on no other evidence than a letter obtained nobody knew how. To *me* the proof was conclusive, and it made me frantic to find that it was not so received by others."

"What did he say when you told him that you had this evidence? How did he act?"

"He swore it was a conspiracy and declared that now he had borne enough of such contumelious conduct that he should soon bring me into subjection. He represented himself to me as an injured and long-suffering man, and me, to myself, as an unkind, undutiful, and most unwomanly woman. He told me, what was true, that I need not expect people to believe such a 'cock and bull story,' and used every possible means of intimidation, except actual corporeal punishment. *That* he threatened long after, and I told him if he ever laid a finger on me, I should certainly shoot him dead. But we had not come to that yet."

"Long after!" I repeated. "You do not, you cannot mean that this wretch continued to live under the same roof with you long after he knew that you would never acknowledge him as your husband?"

"Yes, for years! For years after he knew that I knew he was *what he was,* he lived in my house and took my earnings, yes, and ordered me about and insulted me as much as he liked."

"But," I said, "I cannot understand such a condition of things. Was there no law in the land? No succor in the society about you? How could other women hold still and know that a young creature like you was being tortured in that way?"

"The inertia of women in each other's defense is immense," returned Mrs. Greyfield, in her most incisive tone. "You must not forget that Portland was then almost a wilderness, and families were few and often 'far between.' Among the few, my acquaintances were still fewer, for I had come among them poor and alone, and with all I could do to support myself, without time or disposition to visit. The peculiar circumstances I have related to you broke my spirit and inclined me to seclusion. However, I did carry my evidence and my story together to two or three women who I knew, and what do you suppose they said? That I should have thought of all that before I married! They treated it exactly as if, having gone through the marriage ceremony, I was bound, no matter how many wives Mr. Seabrook had back in Ohio."

"They could not have believed your story," I said, not being able to take in such inferior morality.

"What they believed I do not know; what they said I have told you. I incline to the opinion that they thought I might be a little daft—I am sure I must have looked so at times, from sheer sleeplessness and exhaustion. Or they thought I had no chance of establishing the truth and would be better off to submit quietly. At all events, not one encouraged me to resist Mr. Seabrook, and to overflow my cup of misery, he contrived to find the important letter, which I had hidden, and destroy it."

"Did you never go to men about your case and ask for assistance?"

"At first I was afraid to appeal to them, having had so many unpleasant experiences, and when I at last was driven to seek counsel, I was too late, as I before explained."

"Too late?"

"Yes, I mean that the idea of my being Mr. Seabrook's wife was so firmly seated in their minds that they could not see it in any other light. The fact of my having written and received a letter did not impress them as of any consequence. You will find this to be a truth among men; they respect the sense of ownership of women entertained by each other, and they respect it so much that they would as soon be caught stealing as seeming in any way to interfere with it. That is the reason that, although there is nothing in the wording of the marriage contract converting the woman into a bond slave or a chattel, the man who practices any outrage or wrong on his wife is so seldom called to account. In the eyes of these men, having entered into marriage with Mr. Seabrook, I belonged to him, and there was no help for me. For life and until death I was his to do what he pleased with, so long as he did not bruise my flesh nor break my bones. Is not that an awful power to be lodged with any human being?"

"But," I said, "if they were told the whole truth, that the marriage had never been consummated and why, would they not have been moved by a feeling of chivalry to interfere? Your view of their sentiments presupposes the nonexistence of what I should call chivalry."

"There may be in men such a sentiment as you would call chivalry, but I never yet have seen the occasion where they were pleased to exercise it. I would not advise any other young woman to tell one of them that she had lived alone in the same house with a man reputed to be her husband for seven months without the marriage having been consummated. She would find, as I did, that his chivalry would be exhibited by an ineffectual effort to suppress a smile of incredulity."

"Can it be possible," I was forced to exclaim, "that there was no help for you?"

"You see how it was. I have outlined the bare facts to you. Nobody wanted to be mixed up in my troubles, and the worst of it was that Mr. Seabrook got more sympathy than I did, as the unfortunate husband of a terrible termagant who made his life a burden to him. He could talk in a certain way among men and put on an aggrieved air at home before the boarders. What was the use of my saying anything? If it had not been for my little German neighbor, I should have felt utterly forsaken by all the world. But she, whatever she thought of my domestic affairs, was sorry for me. 'What for you cry so much all de time?' she said to me one day. 'You makes yourself sick all de time mit cryin', an' your face be gettin' wite as my hankershif. De leedle boy, too, he sees you, an' he gets all so wite as you are, all de same. Dat is not goot. You gomes to see me en' brings de boy to see my Hans. You get sheered up den.' And I took her advice for Benton's sake."

"What object had Mr. Seabrook in remaining where he was so unwelcome? He certainly entertained no hope that you would finally yield, and his position could not have been an agreeable one from any point of view; for whether he was regarded as the monster he was or only as a sadly beshrewed husband, he must have felt himself the subject of unpleasant remark."

42

"He could afford to be remarked upon when he was a free pensioner upon a woman's bounty and in receipt of a fine income, which I earned for him by ceaseless toil. I can see him now, sitting at the bottom of the table, my table, flourishing his white hands and stroking his flowing blonde beard occasionally as something very gratifying to his vanity was said, talking and laughing with perfect unconcern while he fattened himself at my expense, while I, who earned and prepared his dinner for him, gasped half-fainting in the heat of a kitchen, sick in heart and body. Do you wonder that I hated him?"

"I wonder more that you did not kill him," I said, feeling that this would have been a case of 'justifiable homicide.'

"The impulse certainly came to me at times to kill him, or if not exactly that, to wish him dead. Yet when the opportunity came to be revenged upon him by fate itself, I interfered to save him. That was strange, was it not? To be suffering as I suffered at this man's hands, and yet when he was in peril to have compassion upon him?"

"You could not alter your nature," I said, "which is, as I told you before, thoroughly sound and sweet. It goes against us to suffer wrong, but it goes still harder with us to do wrong. Besides, you had your religious training to help you."

"I had the temptation, all the same. It happened in this way: One night I was lying awake, as I usually did, until I heard Mr. Seabrook come in and go to his room. He came in rather later than usual, and I listened until all was still in the house, that I might sleep the more safely and soundly afterwards. I had, however, become so nervously wakeful by this time that the much needed and coveted sleep refused to visit me, and I laid tossing feverishly upon my bed when I became aware that there was a smell of fire in the air. Rapidly dressing, I took Benton in my arms and hastened downstairs, to have him where I could save him, should the house be in danger. There was a still stronger odor of burning cloth and wood in the lower rooms, but very little smoke to be detected.

After looking into the kitchen and finding it all right there, I feared the fire might be in the other part of the house and was about to give the alarm, when it occurred to me that the trouble might be in Mr. Seabrook's room.

"Leaving Benton asleep on the dining room table, I ran to his door and knocked. No answer came, but I could smell the smoke within. Pushing open the door I discovered him lying in a perfectly unconscious state and half-undressed on the bed, sleeping off the effects of a wine supper. A candle which he had lighted and left burning had consumed itself down to the socket, and by some chance had ignited a few loose papers on the table beside the bed; the fire had communicated to the bedding on one side and to some of his wearing apparel on the other. All was just ready to burst into a blaze with the admission of fresh air, which I had the presence of mind to prevent, by closing the door behind me.

"There I was, in the presence of my enemy, and he in the clutches of death. I shudder when I think of the feelings of that moment. An evil spirit plainly said to me, 'Now you shall have rest. Let him alone; he is dying by his own hand, not yours—why do you interfere with the decree of fate?' An exulting yet consciously guilty joy agitated my heart, which was beating violently. 'Let him die!' I said to myself, 'let him die!'

"Very rapidly such thoughts whirl through the brain under great excitement. The instant that I hesitated seemed an age of cool deliberation to me. Then the wickedness of my self-gratulation rushed into my mind, making me feel like a murderer. 'O, God,' I cried in anguish of spirit, 'why have I been put to this test?' The next instant I was working with might and main to extinguish the fire, which with the aid of blankets and a pitcher of water was soon suppressed.

"Through it all he slept on, breathing heavily, an object of disgust to my senses and my feelings. When all was safe I returned to my room, thankful that I had been able on the spot to expiate my murderous impulses. The next day he took occasion to say to me, 'I shouldn't have expected a visit of mercy from you, Mrs. Seabrook. If I had known you were coming, I should have tried to keep awake!'

'If ever you refer to such a subject again,' I replied, 'I will set fire to you myself and let you burn,' and either the threat deterred him, or some spark of generosity in his nature was struck by the benefit received, but he never afterwards offered me any annoyance of that kind."

"How did Mr. Seabrook usually treat your son? Was he kind to him?"

"He was not unkind. Perhaps you cannot understand such a character, but he was one who would be kind to man, woman, or child who would be governed by him; yet resistance to his will, however just, roused a tyranny that sought for opportunities to exhibit itself. Such a one passes in general society for a 'good fellow,' because 'the iron hand in the velvet glove' is scarcely perceptible there, while its ungloved force is felt most heavily in the relations of private life. If I had been in a position to flatter Mr. Seabrook, undoubtedly he would have shown me a corresponding consideration, notwithstanding his selfishness. It would have been one way of gratifying his own vanity, by putting me in a humor to pander to it. But knowing how I hated and despised him, he felt toward me all the rancor of his vain and tyrannical nature. It is always more dangerous to hate justly than unjustly, and that is the reason why domestic differences are so bitter. Somebody has always done wrong and knows it, and cannot bear to suffer the natural consequences—the disapprobation of the injured party, in addition to the stings of conscience."

"I suppose, then," I said, "it has been the perception of this truth that has caused the sweetest and purest women in all time to ignore the baser sins of man, while calling their own sex to strict account. And yet I cannot think but that this degree of mercy is injurious to their own purity and derogatory to their dignity. I remember being excessively shocked several years ago by having this trait of *forgiveness* in woman placed in its true light by an accidental publication in a New York paper, which was intended to have just the opposite effect. It was headed 'A Model Woman,' and appeared in the *Evening Post* —Bryant's paper. With a curious desire to know the poet's model for a woman—though the article may have never come under his eye—I commenced reading it. It ran to this effect: a certain man in New York had a good wife and two interesting little children. But he met and fell in love with a handsome, dashing, and rather coarse girl, and the affair had gone so far as to lead to serious expostulation on the part of the wife. The writer did not relate whether or not the girl knew the man to be married, but only that the two were infatuated with each other.

"As the story ran, the wife expostulated and the husband was firm in his determination to possess the girl at all hazards, concluding his declaration with this business statement: 'I shall take the girl and go to California. If you keep quiet about it, I will leave a provision for you and the children; if you do not, I shall go just the same, but without leaving you anything.' *The wife acquiesced to the terms.* Her husband went to California with his paramour, and tired of her (it was in old steamer times), about as soon as he got there. Very soon he deserted her and returned to New York *a la prodigal,* and was received back to the arms of his forgiving wife. The girl followed her faithless lover to New York and, failing to win a kind word from him by the most piteous appeals, finally committed suicide at her hotel in that city. The wife continues to live with the author of this misery upon the most affectionate terms.

"That was the whole story. Is it possible, I asked myself, that the writer of that article, whoever he may be, could have meant its title in anything but irony? Yet, there it stood on the front page of a most respectable journal, endorsed by an editor of the highest reputation. To my way of thinking, the wife was accessory to the crime; had no womanly self-respect, no delicacy, no Christian feelings for her husband's victim; was, in short, morally as guilty as he was; and yet a newspaper of high standing made her out to be a model for wives. For what? Plainly for consenting to or for forgiving three of the most heinous crimes in the decalogue because they were committed *by her husband*. I confess that since that day I have been prone to examine into the claims of men to be forgiven, or the moral right of women to forgive them certain offenses.

"When you examine into the motives of women," said Mrs. Greyfield, "I think you will find there is a large measure of sordid self-interest in their mercy, as in the case you have just quoted. While some women are so weak and so foolishly fond of the men to whom they became early attached as to be willing to overlook everything rather than part with them, a far greater number yield an unwilling submission to wrongs imposed upon them simply because they do not know how to do without the pecuniary support afforded them by their husbands. The bread-and-butter question is demoralizing to women as well as to men, the difference being that men have a wider field to be demoralized in, and that the demoralization of women is greatly consequent upon their circumscribed field of action."

"Do you think that the enlargement of a woman's sphere of work would have a tendency to elevate her moral influence?"

"The way the subject presents itself to me is that it is degrading to have sex determine everything for us: our employments, our position in society, the obedience we owe to others, the influence we are permitted to exercise, all and everything to be dependent upon the delicate matter of a merely physical function. It affects me so unpleasantly to hear such frequent reference to a physiological fact that I have often wished the word *female* stricken from our literature. And when you reflect that we are born and bred to this narrow view of ourselves, as altogether the creatures of sex, you cannot but recognize its belittling, not to say depraving, effect or fail to see the temptation; we have to seize any base advantage it may give us."

When we had canvassed this interesting (to us) topic a little further, I begged Mrs. Greyfield to go on with the relation of her history.

"I find I must be less particular," she said, "to give so many and frequent explanations of my feelings. By this time you can pretty well imagine them, and my story is likely to be too long unless I abbreviate.

"I had been living in the way I have described for two years and had learned to do a good many things in my own defense, very disagreeable to me, but nevertheless very useful. I had gotten a little money together by asking some of my boarders for pay before payday came, or by making such remarks as prompted them to hand the money to me instead of Mr. Seabrook. It was my intention to save enough in such ways to take me to California, where I felt confident, with the experience I had gained, that I should be able to make myself a competence. This plan I had nourished in secret for more than a year when I was tempted to do a very unwise thing.

"I ought to say, perhaps, that with every year that had passed since my arrival in Portland, the population had increased, and with this increase there was a proportionate rise in the value of property. Hearing business topics discussed almost every day at table, I could not help being more or less infected with the spirit of speculation, and it often almost drove me wild to think how profitably I might have invested my earnings could I have gained possession of them for myself.

"Having an opportunity one day to speak on the subject to a gentleman in whose honor I placed great confidence, I mentioned that I was tempted to buy some property, but that my means were so limited I feared I could not do so. He immediately said that he would sell me a certain very good piece of land in the best business locality on the installment plan, and at a bargain, so that when it was paid up I could immediately sell again at an advance. Thinking this would accelerate the carrying out of my scheme of fleeing from my master to a land of freedom, I eagerly accepted the proposition and paid down all the money I had, taking a bond for a deed. The transaction was to be kept a secret between us, and he was to assist me in selling when it came the proper time by deeding direct to my purchaser. I felt almost lighthearted in view of the fact that I should be able, after all, to achieve a kind of independence in the course of time."

"It seems to me," I said, "that I should have grown reckless before this and have done something of a desperate nature—committed suicide, for instance. Did the thought never occur to you to end your bondage in that way?"

"My desperation never took that form, because I had my child to take care of. If I killed myself, I should have to kill him, too. But many and many a night I felt it so impossible to be alive in the morning and go right on in my miserable round of life, worn out in mind and body, with Benton always ailing—often very ill—that I have prepared both myself and him for burial and laid down praying God to take us both before another day. But Death is like our other friends—he is not at hand to do us a service when most desired.

"I have told you that I used to cry a good deal. Weeping, though a relief to us in one way, by removing the pressure upon the brain, is terribly exhausting when excessive, and I was very much wasted by it. An incident occurred about the time I was just speaking of, which gave me comfort in a strange manner. I used sometimes, when my work for the day was done, to leave Benton with my German friend and go out for a walk or to call on an acquaintance. All the sights and sounds of nature are beautiful and beneficial to me in a remarkable degree. With trees and flowers and animals, I am happy and at home.

"One evening I set out to make a visit to Mrs.—, my old neighbor, who lived at some distance from me. The path led through the fir forest and, at the time of day when I was at liberty, was dim and gloomy. I walked hurriedly along, fearing darkness would overtake me, and, looking about me as I went, was snatching a hasty pleasure from the contemplation of Nature's beneficence when my foot caught in a projecting root of some tough shrub, and I fell prostrate.

"In good health and spirits I should not have minded the fall, but to me, in my weak condition, every jar to the nervous system affected me seriously. I rose with difficulty and, seating myself upon a fallen tree, burst into tears and wept violently. It seemed as if even the sticks and stones were in league to injure me. Looking back upon my feelings, I can understand how man, in the infancy of the race, attributed power and will to everything in Nature. In his weakness and inexperience, Nature was too strong for him and bruised him continually.

"As I sat weeping with pain and an impotent resentment, a clear sweet voice spoke to me out of the dusky twilight of the woods. *'Don't cry so much!'* it said. Astonishment dried my tears instantly. I looked about me, but no one was near, nor any sound to be heard but the peculiar cry of a bird that makes itself heard in the Oregon woods at twilight only. A calm that I cannot explain came over my perturbed spirit. It was like the heavenly voices heard upon the earth thousands of years ago, in its power to move the heart. It may make you smile for me to say so, but from that hour I regained a degree of cheerfulness that I had not felt since the day of my marriage to Mr. Seabrook. I did not go to Mrs.—'s that evening, but returned home and went to my bed without putting on clothes to be buried in!"

We talked for a little of well-attested instances of similar incidents of the seeming supernatural. Then I said, "And how did your investment turn out?"

"As might have been expected by a more worldly-wise person. After succeeding, almost, I was defeated by the selfishness and indifference of the man I had trusted to help me through with it. He sold out his property, including that bonded to me, when nearly the whole indebtedness was paid, without mentioning his design or giving me an opportunity to complete the purchase. The new proprietor went immediately to Mr. Seabrook, who, delighted with this unexpected piece of fortune, borrowed the small amount remaining to be paid and had the property deeded to himself. A short time after, he sold it at a handsome advance on the price I paid for it, and I had never one dollar of the money. The entire savings of the whole time I had been in a really profitable business went with that unlucky venture."

"You were just as far from getting to California as ever? O, what outrageous abuse of the power society gives men over women!" I exclaimed with vehemence.

"You may imagine I was bitterly disappointed. The lesson was a hard one but salutary. I took no more disinterested advice; I bought no more property. There are too many agents between a woman and the thing she aims at for her ever to attain it without danger of discomfiture. The experience, as you may guess, put me in no amicable mood towards Mr. Seabrook. Just think of it! There were three years I had supported, by my labor, a large family of men, for that is what it amounted to. My money purchased the food they all ate, and I had really received nothing for it except my board and the clothes I worked in. The fault was not theirs; it was Mr. Seabrook's and society's."

"I will tell you what you remind me of," I said. "You are like Penelope and her train of ravenous suitors in the *Odyssey* of Homer."

"In my busy life, I have not had time to read Homer," Mrs. Greyfield replied. "But if any other woman has been so eaten out of house and home as I was, I am sorry for her."

"Homer's Penelope, if we may believe the poet, was in much better circumstances to bear the ravages of her riotous boarders than you were to feed yours gratuitously."

"Talking about suitors," said Mrs. Greyfield, "I was not without those entirely, either. No young mismated woman can escape them, perhaps. The universal opinion among men seems to be that if you do not like the man you have, you *must* like some other one, and each one thinks it is himself."

The piquant tone in which Mrs. Greyfield uttered her observations always provoked a smile. But I caught at an intimation in her speech. "Sometimes," I said, "you speak as if you acknowledged Mr. Seabrook as your husband, and it shocks me unpleasantly."

"I am speaking of things as they appeared to others. In truth, I was as free to receive suitors as ever I had been, but such was not the common understanding, and I resented the advances of men upon the ground that *they* believed themselves to be acting unlawfully, and that they hoped to make me a party to their breaches of law and propriety. I laugh now, in remembering the blunders committed by self-conceit so long ago, but I did not laugh then; it was a serious matter at that time."

"Was Mr. Seabrook jealous in his behavior, fearing you might fancy someone else?"

"Just as jealous as vain and tyrannical men always are when they are thwarted in their designs. No real husband could have been more critical in his observations on his wife's deportment than he was in his remarks on mine. If I could have been guilty of coquetry, the desire to annoy him would have been incentive enough, but I always considered that I could not afford to suffer in my own estimation for the sake of punishing him. When I recall all these things, I take credit to myself for magnanimity, though then I was governed only by my poor uncultivated judgment and my impulses. For instance, Mr. Seabrook fell ill of a fever not long after he appropriated my real estate. Of course, I was as bitter towards him in my heart as it is possible to conceive, but I could not know that he was lying unattended in his room without offering assistance, so, after many struggles with my self to overcome my strong repulsion, I visited him often enough to give him such attentions as were necessary, but not more. I had no intention of raising any false expectations."

"I hope you took advantage of his being confined to his room, to collect board-money," I said.

"I found out, in time, several ways of managing that matter, which I would once have thought inadmissible. When I had begged some money from a boarder, Mr. Seabrook discovered it when payday came, very naturally. He then ordered me to do the marketing. Without paying any attention to the command, I served up at mealtime whatever there was in the house. This brought out murmurs from the boarders and haughty inquiries from the host himself. All the reply I vouchsafed was that what he procured I would cook. In this way I forced him to pay out the money in his possession, at the expense of my character as a good wife and a polite one. He took his revenge in abusive language and occasional fits of destructiveness in the kitchen, which alarmed my little German neighbor more than it did me. So long as he secured all my earnings and deceived people thoroughly as to his conduct, he maintained, before others at least, a gentlemanly demeanor. But this was gradually giving way to the pressure of a constant thorn in his flesh and the consciousness of his own baseness. He could swear, threaten, and almost strike at slight provocation now. He never really attempted the latter, but once, and it was then I told him I should shoot him, if he dared it.

"I ought to say here that in the last year I had two or three families in the house for a short time. I don't know what these real wives thought of me, that I was a termagant probably, but they were not the kind of women I could talk to about myself, and I made no confidences. A plan was maturing in my mind that was to make it a matter of indifference what anyone thought. I had relinquished the idea of getting enough money together to make a sure start in California and was only waiting to have enough to take me out of the country in any way that I could go cheapest. Another necessary point to gain was secrecy. That could not be gained while I was surrounded by boarders, nor while Mr. Seabrook was in the house, and I resolved to be rid of both."

"O," I cried, delighted and relieved, "how did you manage that?"

"I am going to tell you by how simple an expedient. *I starved them out!*"

"How strange that in all those years you never thought of that," I said laughing. "But, then, neither did Homer's heroine, who kept a first-class free boarding house for twice or thrice as long as you. Do tell me how you accomplished the feat of clearing your house."

"It is not quite true that I had not thought of it, but I had not dared to do it. Besides, I wanted to get some money if possible. Perhaps I should not have done it at the time I did, had not a little help come to me in the shape of real friends. I was all the time like a wild bird in a cage, and the continual attempts to escape I was making only bruised my wings. It occurred to me one day to go to a certain minister who had lately come to Portland, and whose looks pleased me, as did his wife's, and tell them my story. This I did.

"Instead of receiving it as fiction, or doubting the strange parts of it in a way to make me wish I had never spoken of them, they manifested the greatest interest and sympathy, and promised me any assistance they could give. This was the first recognition I had gotten from anyone as being what I was: a woman held in bondage, worse than that of African slavery, by a man to whom she owed nothing, and in the midst of a free, civilized, and Christian community. They were really and genuinely shocked, and firmly determined to help me. I told them all the difficulties in the way and of the expedient I had almost decided upon to free my house from everyone; for I thought that when his income stopped, Mr. Seabrook would be forced to go away and seek some other means of living. They agreed with me that there appeared no better way, and I decided to attempt it.

"It did not take long, of course, to drive away the boarders, for they were there only to eat, and when provisions entirely failed or were uncooked, there was nothing to be done but to go where they could be better served. I did not feel very comfortable over it, as many of them were men I liked and respected, whose ill opinion it was disagreeable to incur, even in a righteous cause, and then no woman likes to be the talk of the town, as I knew I must be. The 'town talk,' as it happened, in time suggested my further course to me."

"Pray tell me if Mr. Seabrook followed the boarders, or did he stay and compel you to cook for him?"

"He stayed, but he did not compel me to cook for him. That I peremptorily refused to do. Neither would I buy any supplies. If he wanted a meal, he must go out, get his provisions, and cook them for himself. Then he refused to buy anything to come in the house, lest I should share *his* plenty. This reduced our rations to nothing. I used to take Benton out and buy him good, wholesome food, myself eating as little as would support nature. Occasionally, now that I had time on my hands, I spent a day out among my few visiting acquaintances, and sometimes I took a meal with my German friend. In this way I compelled my former master to look out for himself.

"One night, there not being a mouthful in the house to eat, I went out and bought a loaf of bread and some milk for Benton's breakfast, for I was careful not to risk the child's health as I risked my own. In the morning when I came downstairs, the bread and milk were gone. Mr. Seabrook had breakfasted. 'Bennie' and I could go hungry. And that brings me back to what 'town talk' did for me.

"It soon became noised about that Mr. and Mrs. Seabrook, who had never got on well together, were now going on dreadfully, and that probably there would be a divorce. 'Divorce!' I said, when my new friend, the minister, mentioned it to me, 'divorce from what? How can there be a divorce where there is no marriage?'

'Nevertheless,' he replied, 'it is worth considering. If the society you live in insists that you are married, why not gratify this society and ask its leave to be legally separated from your nominal husband?'

"At first I rebelled strongly against making this tacit admission of a relationship of that kind to Mr. Seabrook. It appeared to me to be a confession of falsehood to those few persons who were in my confidence, some of whom I felt had always half-doubted the full particulars, as being too ugly for belief. And what was quite as unpalatable as the other was that my enemy would rejoice that for once, at least, and in a public record, I should have to confess myself his wife. My friends argued that it could make little difference, as that was the popular understanding already, which nothing could alter, and that so far as Mr. Seabrook was concerned his triumph would be short-lived and valueless. They undertook to procure counsel and stand by me through the trial."

"What complaint did you propose making?" I interrupted.

"'Neglect of support and cruel treatment,' the general charge that is made to cover so many abominable sins, because we women shrink from exposing the crimes we have been in a measure partners to. My attorney assured me that, under the circumstances, Mr. Seabrook would not make any opposition, fearing we might prove the whole if he did so, but would let the case go by default. This was just what he did, and oh, you should have witnessed his abject humility when I at last had the acknowledged right to put him out of my house!

"Up to the time the divorce was obtained, he kept possession of the room he had first taken, on the lower floor, and which I hired an Indian woman to take care of as one of the chores assigned her about the house. For myself, I would not set my foot in it, except on the occasions referred to; but the rent and the care of it, he had free. Such was the moral degradation of the man, through his own acts, that after all that had passed, he actually cried and begged of me the privilege to remain in that room and be taken care of, as he had been used to be."

"What did you answer him?"

"I told him never to darken my door—never to offend my sight again; that I should never be quite happy while his head was above the sod. O, I was very vindictive! And he was as mild as milk. He could not see why I should hate him so, who had always had so high a regard for me. He had never known a woman he admired and loved so much! Even I was astonished at the man's abjectness."

"It is not uncommon in similar cases. Dependence makes anyone more or less mean, but it is more noticeable in men, who by nature and by custom are made independent. And so you were free at last?"

"Free and happy. I felt as light as a bird and wondered why I couldn't fly! I was poor, but that was nothing. My business was broken up, but I felt confidence in myself to begin again. My health, however, was very much broken down, and my friends said I needed change. That, with the desire to quit a country where I had suffered so much, determined me to come to California. It was the land of promise to my husband—the El Dorado he was seeking when he died. I always felt that if I had come here in the first place, my life would have been very different. So, finally, with the help of my kind friends, I came."

"*I* should have felt, with your experience, no courage to undertake life among strangers, and they mostly men."

"On the contrary, I felt armed in almost every point. The fact of being a divorced woman was my only annoyance, but I was resolved to suppress it so far as I was able and to represent myself to be, as I was, the widow of Mr. Greyfield. I took letters from my friends, to use in case of need, and with nothing but my child and money enough to take me comfortably to the mines on the American River, left Oregon forever."

"To behold you as you are now, in this delightful home, it seems impossible that you should have gone through what you describe, and yet there must have been much more before you achieved the success here indicated."

"It was nothing—nothing at all compared with the other. I proceeded direct to the most populous mining town, hired a house, bought furniture on credit, and took boarders again. I kept only first-class boarders, had high prices, and succeeded."

"Did you never have the mining-stock fever, and invest and lose?"

"Not to any dangerous extent. One or two parties, in whose judgment I knew I might confide, indicated to me where to invest, and I fortunately lost nothing, while I made a little. My best mining-stock was a present from a young man who was sick at my house for a long time, and to whom I was attentive. He was an excellent young fellow, and my sympathies were drawn out towards him: alone in a mining-camp sick, and, as I suspected, moneyless. When he was well enough to go away, he confessed his inability to pay up and presented me with several shares in a mine then but little known, saying that it might not be worth the paper it was printed on, but that he hoped it might bring enough to reimburse my actual outlay on his account; the kindness he had received could not be repaid with filthy lucre. A few months afterwards that stock was worth several thousand dollars. I made diligent inquiry for my young friend, but could get no news of him from that day to this. I have been fortunate in everything I have touched since I came to California. Benton grew well and strong, I recovered my health, Fortune's wheel for me seemed to remain in one happy position, and now there seems nothing for me to do but to move slowly and easily down the sunset slope of life to my final rest."

Mrs. Greyfield smiled and sighed, and remarked upon the fact that the hour hand of the clock pointed to two in the morning. "It is really unkind of me to keep you out of bed until such an hour as this," she said, laughing a little, as if we had only been talking of ordinary things. "But I am in the mood, like the 'Ancient Mariner,' and you are as much forced to listen as the 'Wedding Guest.'"

"There is one thing yet I desire to be satisfied about," I replied. "As a woman, I cannot repress my curiosity to know whether, since all the troubles of your early life have been past, you have desired to marry again. Opportunities I know you must have had. What I want to be informed about is your feeling upon this subject, and whether any man has been able to fill your eye or stir your heart."

The first smile my question called up died away, and an introspective look came over Mrs. Greyfield's still handsome face. She sat silent for a little time, which seemed long to me, for I was truly interested in her reply.

"I think," she said at last, "that women who have had anything like my experience are unfitted for married life. Either they are ruined morally and mentally by the terrible pressure, or they become so sharp-sighted and critical that no ordinary man would be able to win their confidence. I believe in marriage; a single life has an incomplete, one-sided aspect, and is certainly lonely." Then rallying, with much of her usual brightness: "Undoubtedly I have had my times of doubt, when I found it hard to understand myself, and still, here I am! Nobody would have me, or I would not have anybody, or both."

"One more question, then, if it is a fair one: Could you love again the husband of your youth, or has your ideal changed?"

Mrs. Greyfield was evidently disturbed by the inquiry. Her countenance altered, and she hesitated to reply.

"I beg your pardon," I said. "I hope you will not answer me if I have been impertinent."

"That is a question I never asked myself," she finally replied. "My husband was all in all to me during our brief married life. His death left me truly desolate, and his memory sacred. But we were both young, and probably he may have been unformed in character, to a great degree, as well as myself. How he would seem now, if he could be restored to me as he was then, I can only half imagine.

What he would now be, if he had lived on, I cannot at all imagine. But let us now go take a wink of sleep. My eyelids at last begin to feel dry and heavy, and you, I am sure, are perishing under the tortures of resistance to the drowsy god."

"The storm is over," I said. "I thought you felt that something was going to happen!"

"It will be breakfast, I suppose. By the way, I must go and put a note under Jane's door, telling her not to have it before half-past nine. There will be a letter from Benton by the morning mail. Good night, or, good morning, and sweet slumber."

"God be with you," I responded, and in twenty minutes I was sleeping soundly.

Not so my hostess, it seems, for when we met again at our ten-o'clock breakfast, she looked pale and distraught, and acknowledged that she had not been able to compose herself after our long talk. The morning was clear and sunny, but owing to the storm of the night, the mail was late getting in, a circumstance which gave her, as I thought, a degree of uneasiness not warranted by so natural a delay.

"You know I told you," she said, trying to laugh off her nervousness, "that something was going to happen!"

"It would be a strange condition of things where nothing did happen," I answered, and just then the horn of the mail carrier sounded, and the lumbering four-horse coach rattled down the street in sight of our windows.

"There," I said, "is your U.S.M. safe and sound, road agents and landslides to the contrary and of no effect."

Very soon our letters were brought us, and my hostess, excusing herself, retired to her room to read hers. Two hours later she sent for me to come to her. I found her lying with a wet handkerchief folded over her forehead and eyes. A large and thick letter laid half open upon a table beside the bed.

"Read that," she said, without uncovering her eyes.

When I had read the letter, "My dear friend," I said, "what *are* you going to do? I hope, after all, this may be good news."

"What *can* I do? What a strange situation!"

"You will wish to see him, I suppose. 'Arthur Greyfield.' You never told me his name was Arthur," I remarked, thinking to weaken the intensity of her feelings by referring to a trifling circumstance.

"Why have I not died before this time?" she exclaimed, unheeding my attempt at diversion. "This is too much, too much!"

"Perhaps there is still happiness in store for you, my dear Mrs. Greyfield," I said. "Strange as is this new dispensation, may there not be a blessing in it?"

She remained silent a long time, as if thinking deeply. "He has a daughter," she at length remarked, "and Benton says she is very sweet and loveable."

"And motherless," I added, not without design. I had meant only to arouse a feeling of compassion for a young girl half-orphaned, but something more than was in my mind had been suggested to hers. She quickly raised herself from a reclining posture, threw off the concealing handkerchief, and gazed intently in my face, while saying slowly, as if to herself, "Not only motherless, but according to law, fatherless."

"Precisely," I answered. "Her mother was in the same relation to Mr. Greyfield that you were in to Mr. Seabrook, but happily she did not know it in her lifetime."

"Nor he—nor he! Arthur Greyfield is not to be spoken of in the same breath with Mr. Seabrook."

The spirit with which this vindication of her former husband was made caused me to smile, in spite of the dramatic interest of the situation. The smile did not escape her notice.

"You think I am blown about by every contending breath of feeling," she said, wearily, "when the truth is, I am trying to make out the right of a case in which there is so much wrong, and it is no easy thing to do."

"But you will find the right of it at last," I answered. "You are
not called upon to decide in a moment upon a matter of such
weight as this. Take time, take rest, take counsel."

"Will you read the letter over to me?" she asked, lying down
again, and preparing to listen by shielding her face with her hands.

The letter of Arthur Greyfield ran as follows:

"My Dear Anna: How strange it seems to me to be writing to
you again! It is like conversing with one returned from another
world; to you, too, no doubt. There is so much to explain, and
some things that perhaps will not ever be explained satisfactorily
to you, that I know not where to begin or what to say. Still Benton
insists on my writing before seeing you, and perhaps this is best.

"To begin at the beginning. When I was left for dead by my
frightened comrades on the plains, I had not died, but was only
insensible, and I do not believe they felt at all sure of my death, for
they left me unburied as if to give me a chance, and deserted me
rather than take any risks by remaining any longer in that place.
How long I laid insensible I do not know. When I came to myself I
was alone, well wrapped up in a large bed quilt and lying on the
ground close by the wagon trail. Nothing was left for my support, if
alive, from which I concluded that they agreed to consider me dead.

"When I opened my eyes again on the wilderness world about
me, the sun was shining brightly and the wind blowing cool from
the near mountains, but I was too much exhausted to stir, and laid
there, kept alive by the pure air alone, until sunset. About that
time of day I heard the tread of cattle coming and the rumbling of
wagons. The shock of joy caused me to faint, in which condition I
was as found by the advance guard of a large train bound for the
mines in California. I need not tell you what all those men did for
me to bring me round, but they were noble fellows and earned my
everlasting gratitude.

"You can imagine that the first thought in my mind was about
you and Benton. When I was able to talk about myself and answer

questions, my new friends, who had laid by for a couple of days on my account, assured me that they should be able to overtake the California train, in which I supposed you were, before they came to the Sierras. But we had accidents and delays, and failed to come up with that train anywhere on the route.

"At last we arrived in the mining country, and my new friends speedily scattered abroad, looking for gold. I was still too feeble to work in the water, washing out, or to dig. I had no money or property of any kind and was obliged to accept any means that offered of earning a subsistence. Meanwhile I made such inquiry as I could under the circumstances and in such a country, but without learning anything of any of my former friends and acquaintances for two years. Before this time, however, my health was restored, notwithstanding great hardships, and being quite successful in mining, I was laying up considerable gold dust.

"About this time a man came into our camp from Oregon. As I was in the habit of inquiring of any newcomer concerning you, and the people in the train you were in, I asked this man if he had ever met a Mrs. Greyfield or any of the others. He replied that he thought there was a woman of my name living in Portland, Oregon, a year or two before—he was sure he had heard of a young widow of that name. I immediately wrote to you at that place, but whether the letter was lost on the way, or whether it was intercepted there (as by some intimations I have from Benton it might have been), no reply ever came to it. I also sent a letter to Mr.—, in whose care I had left you, but nothing was ever heard from him.

"When I had waited a reasonable length of time, I wrote again to the postmaster of the same place, asking him if he knew of such a person as Mrs. Greyfield in Oregon. The reply came this time from a man named Seabrook, who said that there had been a woman of the name of Greyfield in Portland at one time, but that both she and her child were dead. This news put an end to inquiries in that direction, though I continued to look for anyone who might have known you and finally found one of our original party, who confirmed the intelligence of your having gone to Oregon instead of California, and so settled the question, as I supposed, forever.

"You may wonder, dear Anna, that I did not go to Oregon when I had the barest suspicion of your being there. The distance and the trouble of getting there were not what deterred me. I was making money where I was and did not wish to abandon my claim while it was producing well, for an uncertain hint that might mislead me."

"Stop there!" interrupted Mrs. Greyfield. "Do you think *I* should have hesitated in a case like that? But go on."

"I knew you had considerable property, and thought I knew you were with friends who would not let you suffer—"

"Though they had abandoned him while still alive, in the wilderness! Beg pardon, please go on again."

"And that Oregon was really a more comfortable and safe place for a family than California, as times were then—"

Mrs. Greyfield groaned.

"And that you, if there, would do very well until I could come for you. I could not suspect that you would avail yourself of the privilege of widowhood within so short a time, if ever."

"O!" ejaculated my listener, with irrepressible impatience.

I read on without appearing to observe the interruption.

"To tell the truth I had not thought of myself as dead, and that is probably where I made the greatest mistake. It did not occur to me that you were thinking of yourself as a widow; therefore, I did not realize the risk. But when the news came of your death, if it were really you, as I finally made up my mind it must be—"

An indignant gesture, accompanied by a sob, expressed Mrs. Greyfield's state of feeling on this head.

"I fell into a state of confirmed melancholy, reproaching myself severely for not having searched the continent over before stopping to dig gold! Though it was for you I was digging it, and our dear boy, who I believed alive and well somewhere, until I received Mr. Seabrook's letter.

"My dear Anna, I come now to that which will try your feelings, but you must keep in view that I have the same occasion for complaint. Having made a comfortable fortune and feeling miserable about you and the boy, I concluded to return to the Atlantic States to visit my old home. While there I met a lovely and excellent girl, who consented to be my wife, and I was married the second time. We had one child, a girl, now eighteen years of age, and then my wife died. I mourned her sincerely, but not more so than I had mourned you.

"At last, after all these years, news came of you from a reliable source. The very man to whose charge I committed you when I expected to die returned to the States, and from him I heard of your arrival in Oregon, your marriage, and your subsequent divorce. Painful as this last news was to my feelings, I set out immediately for California (I had learned from him that you were probably in this state) and commenced inquiries. An advertisement of mine met Benton's eye only two days ago, and you may imagine my pleasure at the discovery of my only and dear son, so long lost to me. He is a fine, manly fellow and good, for which I have to thank you, of course."

"You see, he appropriates Benton at once. Never so much as 'by your leave.' But Benton will not quit me to follow this newfound father," Mrs. Greyfield said, with much feeling.

"He may not be put to the test of a choice. You have a proposition to consider," I replied. "Let me read it."

"No, no! Yet, read it; what do I care? Go on."

"My daughter, Nellie, is the very picture of her mother, and as sweet and good as one could desire. Benton seems to be delighted with her for a sister. And now that the young folks have taken such a fancy to each other, there is something that I wish to propose to you. It cannot be expected, after all that has passed, and with the lapse of so many years, we could meet as if nothing had come between us—"

"Who suffered all this to come between us?" cried Mrs. Greyfield, much agitated.

"But I trust we can meet as friends, dear friends, and that possibly in time we may be reunited, as much for our own sakes as the children's."

"O, how can I ever forgive him? Does it not seem to you that if Mr. Greyfield had done his duty, all this terrible trouble and illegal marrying would have been avoided? Do you think a man should consider anything in this world before his wife and children, or fail of doing his utmost in any circumstances for them? How else is marriage superior to any illicit relation, if its duties are not sacred and not to be set aside for anything? I could never have done as he has done, blameless as he thinks himself."

The condition of Mrs. Greyfield's mind was as such that no answer was written or attempted that day nor the next. She sent a brief dispatch to Benton, asking him to come home and come alone. I wished to go away, thinking she would prefer being left quite to herself under the circumstances, but she insisted on my remaining until something had been decided on about the meeting between her and Mr. Greyfield. Benton came home as requested, and the subject was canvassed in all its bearings. The decision arrived at was that an invitation should be sent to Mr. Greyfield and his daughter to visit Mrs. Greyfield for a fortnight. Everything beyond that was left entirely to the future. When all was arranged, I took my leave, promising and being promised frequent letters.

The last time I was at Mrs. Greyfield's, I found there only herself and her daughter, Nellie.

"I have adopted her," she said, "with her father's consent. She is a charming girl, and I could not bear to leave her motherless. Benton is very much attached to his father. They are off on a mountaineering expedition at present, but I hope they will come home before you go away."

"Are you not going to tell me," I asked, "how you finally settled matters between Mr. Greyfield and yourself?"

"He is a very persistent suitor," she replied, smiling. "I can hardly tell what to do with him."

"You do not want to break bark over his head?" I said, laughing.

"No, but I do almost wish that since he had stayed away so long he had never come back. I had got used to my own quiet, old-maid ways. I was done, or thought I was done, with passion and romance, and now to be tossed about in this way, on the billows of doubt— to love and not to love, to feel revengeful and forgiving, to think one way in the morning and another way by noon—is very tiresome. I really do *not* know what to do with him."

I smiled because I thought the admission was as good as Mr. Greyfield need desire for his prospects.

"I think I can understand," I said, "how difficult it must be to get over all the gaps made by so many years of estrangement—of fancied death, even. Had you been looking for him for such a length of time, there would still be a great deal of awkwardness in the meeting when you came together again."

"Yes," said Mrs. Greyfield, "it is inevitable. The most artistic bit of truth in the *Odyssey* (you see I have read Homer since you called me Penelope) is where the poet describes the difficulty the faithful wife had in receiving the long-absent, and now changed, Ulysses as her true husband."

"But she did receive him," I interrupted, "and so will you."

"The minister will have to bless the reception then. And to confess the whole truth to you, we are corresponding with my friend of long ago in Portland. He has promised to come down to perform the ceremony, and as his health is impaired, we have invited him to bring his family, at our expense, and to remain in our home while Mr. Greyfield and I, with Benton and Nellie, make a tour to and through Europe."

"How much you and Mr. Greyfield must have to talk over! It will take a year or two of close association to make you even tolerably well acquainted again."

"No, the 'talking over' is *tabooed*, and that is why we are going to travel—to have something else to talk about. You see I am so unforgiving that I cannot bear to hear Mr. Greyfield's story, and too magnanimous, notwithstanding, to inflict mine upon him. To put temptation out of my way, I proposed this European excursion."

"You are commencing a new life," I said. "May it be as happy as your darkest days were sad. There is one thing you never told me, what became of Mr. Seabrook?"

"I saw his death in a Nevada paper only a few days ago. He died old, poor, and alone, or so the account ran, in a cabin among the mountains. 'The mills of the gods,' etc., you know?"

"Then I am not to see Mr. Greyfield?"

"O yes, if you will stay until Mr.— comes from Portland. I shall be glad of your presence on that occasion. Mr. Greyfield, you must understand, is under orders to keep out of the way until that time arrives. You can be of service to me, if you will stay."

I stayed and saw them off to Europe, then went on my way to Lake Tahoe to meet other friends, but I have a promise from this strangely reunited couple to spend a summer in Oregon when they return from their transatlantic tour, at which time I hope to be able to remove from Mrs. Greyfield's mind the painful impression derived from her former acquaintance with the city of my adoption.

How Jack Hastings
Sold His Mine

T he passenger train from the East came thundering down the head of the Humboldt Valley, just as morning brightened over the earth—refreshing eyes wearied with yesterday's mountains and cañons by a vision of green willows and ash trees, a stream that was not a torrent, and a stretch of grassy country.

Among the faces oftenest turned to the flitting views was that of a young, gracefully-formed, neatly-dressed, delicate-looking woman. The large brown eyes often returned from gazing at the landscape to scan with seriousness some memoranda she held in her hand. "Arrive at Elko at eight o'clock A.M.," said the memorandum. Consulting a tiny watch, whose hands pointed to ten minutes of eight, the lady began making those little preparations which betoken the journey's end at hand.

"What a strange-looking place it is!" she thought, as the motley collection of board shanties and canvas houses came in sight—for the famous Chloride District had been discovered but a few months before, and the Pacific Railroad was only four weeks open. "I wish Jack had come to meet me! I'm sure I don't see how I am to find the stage agent to give him Jack's letter. What a number of people!"

This mental ejaculation was called forth by the sight of the long platform in front of the eating house, crowded with a surging mass of humanity just issuing from the dining room. They were the passengers of the eastward-bound train, ready to rush headlong for the cars when the momently-expected "All aboard!" should be shouted at them by the conductor. Into this crowd the freshly arrived passengers of the westward-bound train were a moment after ejected—each eyeing the other with a natural and pardonable interest.

The brown-eyed, graceful young lady conducted herself in a very business-like manner—presenting the checks for her baggage, inquiring out the office of Wells, Fargo & Co., and handing in her letter, all in the briefest possible time. Having secured a seat in a coach to Chloride Hill, with the promise of the agent to call for her when the time for departure arrived, the lady retired to the dining room just in time to see her acquaintances of the train departing. Sitting down alone to a hastily-cooked and underdone repast, she was about finishing a cup of bitter black coffee with a little shudder of disgust when a gentleman seated himself opposite her at table. The glance the stranger cast in her direction was rather a lingering one; then he ordered his breakfast and ate it. Meanwhile, the lady retired to the ladies' sitting room.

After an hour of waiting, one, two, three coaches rolled past the door, and the lady began to fear she had been forgotten when the polite agent appeared to notify "Mrs. Hastings" that "the stage was ready." This was Mrs. Alice Hastings, then-wife of Mr. Jack Hastings, of Deep Cañon, Chloride District. The agent thought Mr. Hastings had a very pretty wife and expressed his opinion in his manner, as men will.

When, just before starting, there entered three of the roughest-looking men she had ever encountered, Mrs. Hastings began to fear that in his zeal to obey instructions, the agent had exceeded them, and in packing the first three coaches with first-comers, had left this one to catch up the fag end of travel. If the first impression, gained from sight, had made her shrink a little, what was her dismay when, at the end of ten minutes, one of her fellow travelers—the only American of the three—produced a bottle of brandy, which, having offered it first to her, he passed to the bullet-headed Irishman and very shabby Jew—repeating the courtesy once every twenty minutes for several times.

Mrs. Hastings was a brave sort of woman, where courage was needful, and she now began to consider the case in hand with what coolness she could command. One hundred and thirty miles— eighteen or twenty hours of such companionship—with no chance of change or intermission, a wilderness country to travel over, and all the other coaches a long way ahead. The dainty denizen of a city home, shuddering inwardly, showed outwardly a serene countenance. Her American friend, with wicked black eyes and a jolly and reckless style of carrying himself, continued to offer brandy at short intervals.

"Best take some, Madame," said he, "this dust will choke you if you don't."

"Thanks," returned the lady, with her sweetest smile, "I could not drink brandy. I have wine in my traveling basket, should I need it, but much prefer water."

At the next station, although hardly four minutes were lost in changing horses, the men procured for her a cup of water. Mrs. Hastings' thanks were frank and cordial. She even carefully opened a conversation about the country they were passing over and contrived to get them to ask a question or two about herself. When they learned that she had come all the way from New York on the newly opened railroad, their interest was at its height, and when they heard that she was going to join her husband in the Chloride District, their sympathy was thoroughly enlisted.

"Wonderful—such a journey! How she could be six days on the cars, and yet able to take such a stage-ride as this, is astonishing."

Such were the American's comments. The Jew thought of the waiting husband—for your Israelite is a man of domestic and family affections. "Her husband looking for her, and she behind time!

How troubled he must be! Didn't he know how it was? Wasn't his wife gone away on a visit once, and didn't write, and he a running to the express office every morning and evening for a letter, and getting so anxious as to telegraph? Such an expense and loss of time—and all because he felt so uneasy about his wife!"

The bullet-headed young Irishman said nothing. He was about half-asleep from brandy and last night's travel; too stupid to know that his hat had flown out of the window and was bowling along in the wind and dust half a mile behind—all the better for his head, which looked at a red heat now.

The lady had lifted the rude men up to her level, when directly they were ashamed of their brandy and other vices, and began to show instinctive traits of gentlemen. By the time they arrived at the dinner station, where half an hour was allowed for food and rest out of the eighteen or twenty, she had at least two humble servitors, who showed great concern for her comfort.

The day began to wane. They had traveled continuously over a long stretch of plain between two mountain ranges, over a country entirely uninhabited, except by the stage company's employees, who kept the stations and tended the stock. This lone woman had seen but one other woman on the road. Plenty of teams—great "prairie schooners," loaded with every conceivable thing for supplying the wants of an isolated, non-producing community, and drawn by ten or fourteen mules—had been passed through the day.

As night fell, Mrs. Hastings saw what she had never before seen or imagined—the camps of these teamsters by the roadside, horses and mules staked or tied to the wagons, the men lying prone upon the earth, wrapped in blankets, their dust-blackened faces turned up to the frosty twinkling stars. Did people really live in that way? How many superfluous things were there in a city!

The night was moonless and clear, and cold as at that altitude they always are. Sleep, from the roughness of the road, was impossible. Her companions dozed and woke with exclamations when the heavy lurchings of the coach disturbed them too roughly. Mrs. Hastings never closed her eyes. When morning dawned, they were on the top of a range of mountains, like those that had been in sight all the day before. Down these heights they rattled away, and at four in the morning, entered the streets of Chloride Hill— a city of board and canvas houses. Arrived at the stage office, the lady looked penetratingly into the crowd of men always waiting for the stages, but saw no face she recognized. Yes, one—and that was the face of the gentleman who sat down opposite her at table in Elko.

"Permit me," he said, "I think you inquired for Mr. Hastings?"

"I did; he is my husband. I expected to find him here," she replied, feeling that sense of injury and desire to cry, which tired women feel, jostled about in a crowd of men.

Leaving her a moment to say something to an employee of the office, the stranger returned immediately, saying to the man: "Take this lady to Mrs. Robb's boardinghouse." Then to her: "I will inquire for your husband, and send him to you if he is in town. The hack does not go over to Deep Cañon for several hours yet. Meanwhile, you had better take some rest. You must be greatly fatigued."

Fatigued! Her head swam round and round, and she really was too much exhausted to feel as disappointed as she might at Jack's non-appearance. Much relieved by the prospect of a place to rest in, she followed the man summoned to escort her, and fifteen minutes after was sound asleep on a sofa of the boardinghouse.

Three hours of sleep and a partial bath did much to restore tired nature's equilibrium, and, although her head still felt absurdly light, Mrs. Hastings enjoyed the really excellent breakfast provided for her, wondering how such delicacies ever got to Chloride Hill. Breakfast over and no news of Jack, the time began to drag wearily. She was more than half-inclined to be angry—only relenting when she remembered that she was two or three days behind time, and of course Jack could not know when to expect her. She had very full directions, and if she could not find her way to Deep Cañon, she was a goose, that was all!

So she sent for the driver of the hack, told him to get her baggage from the express office, and started for Deep Cañon. Who should she find in the hack but her friend of the morning!

"I could not hear of your husband," said he, "but you are sure to find him at home."

Mrs. Hastings smiled faintly and hoped she should. Then she gave her thoughts to the peculiar scenery of the country and to the sharpness of the descent as they whirled rapidly down the four miles of cañon, at the bottom of which was the town of that name—another one of those places which had "come up as a flower" in a morning. She longed to ask about her husband and his "home," but as there were several persons in the stage, she restrained her anxiety and said never a word until they stopped before the door of a saloon where all the other passengers alighted. Then she told the driver she wanted to be taken to Mr. Hastings' house.

He didn't know where that was, he said, but would inquire.

Did he know Dr. Earle?

"That's him, ma'am," pointing out her friend of the morning.

"How can I serve you?" he asked, raising his hat politely.

Mrs. Hastings blushed rosily, between vexation at Jack's invisibility and confusion at being so suddenly confronted with Dr. Earle.

"Mr. Hastings instructed me to inquire of you, if I had any difficulty in finding him," she said apologetically.

"I will show you his place with pleasure," returned the doctor pleasantly, and, jumping on the box, proceeded to direct the driver.

Had ladies of Mrs. Hastings' style been as plenty in Deep Cañon as in New York, the driver would have grumbled at the no road he had to follow along the stony side of a hill and among the stumps of mahogany trees. But there were few like her in that mountain town, and his chivalry compelled him to go out of his way with every appearance of cheerfulness. Presently, the stage stopped where the sloping ground made it very uncertain how long it could maintain its balance in that position, and the voice of Dr. Earle was heard saying, "This is the place."

Mrs. Hastings, who had been looking out for some sign of home, was seized with a doubt of the credibility of her senses. It was on the tip of her tongue to say, "This must be the house of some other Mr. Hastings," when she remembered prudence and said nothing. Getting out and going toward the house to inquire, the door opened, and a man in a rough mining suit came quickly forward to meet her.

"Alice!"

"Jack!"

Dr. Earle and the driver studiously looked the other way while salutations were exchanged between Mr. and Mrs. Hastings. When they again ventured a look, the lady had disappeared within the cabin, the first glimpse of which had so dismayed her.

That afternoon, Jack initiated Alice into the mysteries of cooking by an open fire and expatiated largely on the merits of his outside kitchen. Alice hinted to him that she was accustomed to sleep on something softer than a board, and the two went together to a store to purchase materials out of which to make a mattress.

After that, for two or three weeks, Mrs. Hastings was industriously engaged in wondering what her husband meant when he wrote that he had built a house and was getting things ready to receive her. Reason or romance as she might, she could not make that single room of rough boards, roofed with leaky canvas and unfurnished with a single comfort of life, into a house or home. At last, Jack seemed to guess her thoughts, for she never spoke them.

"If I could sell my mine," he then often said, "I could fix things up."

"If you sold your mine, Jack, you would go back to New York, and then there would be no need of fixing up this place." Alice wanted to say "horrid" place, but refrained.

At length, from uncongenial air, water, food, and circumstances in general, the transplanted flower began to droop. The great heat and rarefied mountain air caused frantic headaches, aggravated by the glare which came through the white canvas roof. Then came the sudden mountain tempests, when the rain deluged everything, and it was hard to find a spot to stand in where the water did not drip through. She grew wild, looking forever at bare mountainsides simmering in the sun by day, and at night over their tops up to the piercing stars. A constant anxious fever burnt in her blood that the cold night air could not quench, though she often left her couch to let it blow chilly over her in her loose night robes. Then she fell really ill.

Sitting by her bedside, Jack said, "If I could sell my mine!" And she had answered, "Let the mine go, Jack, and let us go home. Nothing is gained by stopping in this dreadful place."

Then Mr. Hastings had replied to her, "I have no money, Alice, to go home with; not a cent. I borrowed ten dollars of Earle today to buy some fruit for you."

That was the last straw that broke the camel's back. By night Mrs. Hastings was delirious, and Dr. Earle was called.

"She has a nervous fever," he said, "and needs the carefullest nursing."

"Which she cannot have in this d—d place," Mr. Hastings replied, profanely.

"Why don't you try to get something to do?" asked Earle of the sad-visaged husband, a day or two after.

"What is there to do? Everything is flat; there is neither business nor money in this cursed country. I've stayed here trying to sell my mine, until I'm dead broke; nothing to live on here, and nothing to get out with. What I'm to do with my wife there, I don't know.

Let her die, perhaps, and throw her bones up that ravine to bleach in the sun. God! What a position to be in!"

"But you certainly must propose to do something, and that speedily. Couldn't you see it was half that that brought this illness on your wife; the inevitable which she saw closing down upon you?"

"If I cannot sell my mine soon, I'll blow out my brains, as that poor German did last week. Alice heard the report of the shot which killed him, and I think it hastened on her sickness."

"And so you propose to treat her to another such scene and put an end to her?" said Earle savagely.

"Better so than to let her starve," Jack returned, growing pale with the burden of possibilities that oppressed him. "How the devil I am to save her from that last, I don't know. There is neither business, money, nor credit in this infernal town. I've been everywhere in this district, asking for a situation at something, and cannot get anything better than digging ground on the new road."

"Even that might be better than starving," said Dr. Earle.

Jack was a faithful nurse, Dr. Earle an attentive physician. Young people with elastic constitutions die hard, so Alice began to mend and in a fortnight was convalescent. Jack got a situation in a quartz mill where the doctor was part owner.

Left all day alone in the cabin, Alice began staring again at the dreary mountains, whose walls inclosed her on every side. The bright scarlet and yellow flowers that grew out of their parched soil sometimes tempted her to a brief walk, but the lightness of the air fatigued her, and she did not care to clamber after them.

One day, being lonely, she thought to please Jack by dressing in something pretty and going to the mill to see him. So, laying aside the wrapper which she had worn almost constantly lately, she robed herself in a delicate linen lawn, donned a coquettish little hat and parasol, and set out for the mill, a mile away. Something in the thought of the pleasant surprise it would be to Jack gave her strength and animation, and though she arrived somewhat out of breath, she looked as dainty and fresh as a rose, and Jack was immensely proud and flattered. He introduced her to the head of the firm, showed her over the mill, pointed out to her the mule train packing wood for the engine fires, got the amalgamator to give her specimens, and in every way showed his delight.

After an hour or so, she thought about going home, but the walk home looked in prospect very much longer than the walk to the mill. In truth, it was harder by reason of being uphill. But opportunely, as it seemed, just as Jack was seeing her off the door-stone of the office, Dr. Earle drove up and, comprehending the situation, offered to take Mrs. Hastings to her own door in his carriage, if she would graciously allow him five minutes to see the head man in.

When they were seated in the carriage, a rare luxury in Deep Cañon, and had driven a half mile in embarrassed silence—for Mrs. Hastings somehow felt ashamed of her husband's dependence upon this man—the doctor spoke, and what he said was this:

"Your life is very uncongenial to you; you wish to escape from it, don't you?"

"Yes, I wish to escape; that is the word which suits my feeling—a very strange feeling it is."

"Describe it," said the doctor, almost eagerly.

"Ever since I left the railroad, in the midst of a wilderness and borne for so many hours away into the heart of still more desert wilderness, my consciousness of things has been very much confused. I can only with difficulty realize that there is any such place as New York, and San Francisco is a fable. The world seems a great bare mountain plane, and I am hanging on to its edge by my fingertips, ready to drop away into space. Can you account for such impressions?"

"Easily, if I chose. May I tell you something?"

"What is it?"

"I've half a mind to run away with you."

Now, as Dr. Earle was a rather young and a very handsome man, had been very kind, and was now looking at her with eyes actually moistened with tears, a sudden sense of being on the edge of a pitfall overcame Mrs. Hastings, and she turned pale and red alternately. Yet, with the instinct of a pure woman, to avoid recognizing an ugly thought, she answered with a laugh as gay as she could make it.

"If you were a witch, and offered me half of your broomstick to New York, I don't know but I should take it—that is, if there was room on it anywhere for Jack."

"There wouldn't be," said the doctor, and said no more.

The old fever seemed to have returned that afternoon. The hills glared so that Mrs. Hastings closed the cabin door to shut out the burning vision. The ground squirrels, thinking from the silence that no one was within, ran up the mahogany tree at the side and scampered over the canvas roof in glee. One, more intent on gain than the rest, invaded Jack's outside kitchen, knocking down the dishes with a clang and scattering the dirt from the turf roof over the flour sack and the two white plates. Every sound made her heart beat faster. Afraid of the silence and loneliness at last, she reopened the door, and then a rough-looking man came to the entrance to inquire if there were any silver leads up the ravine.

Leads? She could not say. Prospectors in plenty there were.

Then he went his way, having satisfied his curiosity, and the door was closed again. Some straggling donkeys wandered near, which were mistaken for "diggers," and dreading their glittering eyes, the nervous prisoner drew the curtain over the one little sliding window. There was nothing to read, nothing to sew, no housekeeping duties, because no house to keep; she was glad when the hour arrived for preparing the late afternoon meal.

That night she dreamed that she was a skeleton lying up the cañon—the sunshine parching her naked bones; that Dr. Earle came along with a pack train going to the mill, and picking her up carefully, laid her on top of a bundle of wood; that the Mexican driver covered her up with a blanket, which so smothered her that she awakened and started up gasping for breath. The feeling of suffocation continuing, she stole softly to the door and, opening it, let the chilly night air blow over her. Most persons would have found Mr. Hastings' house freely ventilated, but some way poor Alice found it hard to breathe in it.

The summer was passing; times grew, if possible, harder than before. The prospectors, who had found plenty of "leads," had spent their "bottom dollar" in opening them up and in waiting for purchasers, and were going back to California any way they could. The capitalists were holding off, satisfied that in the end all the valuable mines would fall into their hands and caring nothing how fared the brave but unlucky discoverers. In fact, they overshot themselves and made hard times for their own mills, the miners having to stop getting out rock.

Then Jack lost his situation. Very soon food began to be scarce in the cabin of Mr. Hastings. Scanty as it was, it was more than Alice craved; or rather, it was not what she craved. If she ate for a day or two, for the next two or three days she suffered with nausea and aversion to anything which the outside kitchen afforded. Jack seldom mentioned his mine now, and looked haggard and hopeless. The conversation between her husband and Dr. Earle, recorded elsewhere, had been overheard by Alice, lying half-conscious, and she had never forgotten the threat about blowing out his brains in case he failed to sell his mine. Trifling as such an apprehension may appear to another, it is not unlikely that it had its effect to keep up her nervous condition. The summer was going—was gone. Mrs. Hastings had not met Dr. Earle for several weeks, and, despite herself, when the worst fears oppressed her, her first impulse was to turn to him. It had always seemed so easy for him to do what he liked!

Perhaps he was growing anxious to know if he could give the thumbscrew another turn. At all events, he directed his steps toward Mr. Hastings' house on the afternoon of the last day in August. Mrs. Hastings received him at the threshold and offered him the camp stool—the only chair she had—in the shade outside the door, at the same time seating herself upon the doorstep with the same grace as if it had been a silken sofa.

She was not daintily dressed this afternoon, for that luxury, like others, calls for the expenditure of a certain amount of money, and money Alice had not—not even enough to pay a Chinaman for "doing up" one of her pretty muslins. Neither had she the facilities for doing them herself, had she been skilled in that sort of labor, for even to do your own washing and ironing presupposes the usual conveniences of a laundry, and these did not belong to the furniture of the outside kitchen. She had not worn her linen lawn since the visit to the mill. The dust which blew freely through every crack of the shrunken boards precluded such extravagance. Thus it happened that a soiled cashmere wrapper was her afternoon wear. She had faded a good deal since her coming to Deep Cañon, but still looked pretty and graceful, and rather too *spirituelle*.

The doctor held in his hand, on the point of a knife, the flower of a cactus very common in the mountains, which he presented her, warning her at the same time against its needlelike thorns.

"It makes me sick," said Alice hastily, throwing it away. "It is the color of gold, which I want so much, and of the sunshine, which I hate so."

"I brought it to you to show you the little emerald bee that is always to be found in one—it is wondrously beautiful—a living gem, is it not?"

"Yes, I know," Alice said, "I admired the first one I saw, but I admire nothing any longer—nothing at least which surrounds me here."

"I understand that, of course," returned the doctor. "It is because your health is failing you—because the air disagrees with you."

"And because my husband is so unfortunate. If he could only get away from here—and I!" The vanity of such a supposition, in their present circumstances, brought the tears to her eyes and a quiver about her mouth.

"Why did you ever come here! Why did he ever ask you to come—how *dared* he?" demanded the doctor, setting his teeth together.

"That is a strange question, doctor!" Mrs. Hastings answered with dignity, lifting her head like an antelope. "My husband was deceived by the same hopes that have ruined others. If I suffer, it is because we are both unfortunate."

"What will he do next?" questioned the doctor curtly. The cruel meaning caused the blood to forsake her cheeks.

"I cannot tell what he will do"—her brief answer rounded by an expressive silence.

"You might help him. Shall I point out the way to you?"—watching her intently.

"Can you? Can I help him?"—her whole form suddenly inspired with fresh life.

Dr. Earle looked into her eager face with a passion of jealous inquiry that made her cast down her eyes:

"Alice, do you love this Hastings?"

He called her Alice; he used a tone and asked a question which could not be misunderstood. Mrs. Hastings dropped her face in her hands, her hands upon her knees. She felt like a wild creature which the dogs hold at bay. She knew now what the man meant and the temptation he used.

"Alice," he said again, "this man, your husband, possesses a prize he does not value, or does not know how to care for. Shall you stay here and starve with him? Is he worth it?"

"He is my husband," she answered simply, lifting up her face; calm, if mortally pale.

"And I might be your husband, after a brief interval," he said quickly. "There would have to be a divorce—it could be conducted quietly. I do not ask you to commit yourself to dishonor. I will shield you; no care shall fall upon you, nor any reproach. Consider this well, dearest darling Alice, and what will be your fate if you depend upon him."

"Will it help him then, to desert him?" she asked faintly.

"Yes, unless by remaining with him you can insure his support. Maintain you he cannot. Suppose his mine were sold, he would waste that money as he wasted what he brought here. I don't want his mine, yet I will buy it tomorrow if that will satisfy you, and have your promise to go with me. I told you once that I wanted to run away with you, and now I mean to. Shall I tell you my plan?"

"No, not today," Mrs. Hastings answered, struggling with her pain and embarrassment, "I could not bear it today, I think."

"How cruel I am while meaning to be kind! You are agitated as you ought not to be in your weak state. Shall I see you tomorrow—professional visit, you know?"

"You will buy the mine?"—faintly, with something like a blush.

"Certainly; I swear I will—on what conditions, you know."

"On none other?"

"Shall I rob myself, not of money only, but of what is far dearer? On none other." He rose, took her cold hand, clasped it fervently, and went away.

When Jack came home to his very meagre dinner, he brought a can of peaches, which, being opened, looked so deliciously cool and tempting that Alice could not refrain from volubly exulting over them. "But how did you get them, Jack?" she asked, "Not by going into debt, I hope."

"No. I was in Scott's store, and Earle, happening to come in just as Scott was selling some and praising them highly, paid for a can and asked me to take them to you and get your opinion. They are splendid, by Jove!"

"I do not fancy them," said Alice, setting down her plate. "But don't tell the doctor," she added hastily.

"You don't fancy anything, lately, Alice," Mr. Hastings replied, rather crossly.

"Never mind, Jack. My appetite will come when you have sold your mine." And upon that, the unreasonably fastidious woman burst into tears.

"As if my position is not trying enough without seeing you cry!" said Jack, pausing from eating long enough to look injured. Plastic Jack! Your surroundings were having their effect on you.

The *Mining News* of the second of September had a notice of the sale of Mr. Hastings' mine, the "Sybil," bearing chloride of silver, to Dr. Eustance Earle, all of Deep Cañon. The papers to be handed over and cash paid down at Chloride Hill on the seventh, at which time Dr. Earle would start for San Francisco on the business of the mining firm to which he belonged. Mr Hastings, it was understood, would go east about the same time.

All the parties were at Chloride Hill on the morning of the seventh, promptly. By eleven o'clock, the above-mentioned transaction was completed. Shortly after, one of the Opposition Line's stages stopped at Mrs. Robb's boardinghouse, and a lady, dressed for traveling, stepped quickly into it. Having few acquaintances and being closely veiled, the lady passed unrecognized at the stage office, where the other passengers got in.

Half an hour afterwards, Mr. Jack Hastings received the following note:

> DEAR JACK: I sold your mine for you. Dr. Earle is running away with me, per agreement. But if you take the express this afternoon, you will reach Elko before the train leaves for San Francisco tomorrow. There is nothing worth going back for at Deep Cañon. If you love me, save me.
>
> Devotedly, ALICE

It is superfluous to state that Jack took the express, which, arriving at Elko before the Opposition, made him master of the situation. Not that he felt very masterful; he didn't. He was thinking of many things that it hurt him to remember, but he was meaning to do differently in the future. He had at last sold his mine—no, he'd be d—d if *he* had sold it, but—Hallo! There's a big dust out on the road there—it must be the other stage. Think what you'll do and say, Jack Hastings!

What he did say was: "Ah, doctor! You here? It was lucky for my wife, wasn't it, since I got left, to have you to look after her? Thanks, old fellow, you are just in time for the train. Alice and I will stop over a day to rest. A thousand times obliged: good-bye! Alice, say good-bye to Doctor Earle! You will not see him again."

Their hands and eyes met. He was pale as marble. She flushed one instant, paled the next, with a curious expression in her eyes, which the doctor never forgot and never quite understood. It was enough to know that the game was up. He had another mine on his hands and an ugly pain in his heart, which he told himself bitterly would be obstinate of cure. If he only could be sure what that look in her eyes had meant!

SAM RICE'S ROMANCE

The coach of Wells, Fargo & Co. stood before the door of Piney-woods Station, and Sam Rice, the driver, was drawing on his lemon-colored gloves with an air, for Sam was the pink of stage-drivers, from his high white hat to his faultless French boots. Sad will it be when his profession shall have been altogether superseded, and the coach-and-six, with its gracious and graceful "whip," shall have been supplanted, on all the principal lines of travel, by the iron horse with its grimy "driver" and train of thundering carriages.

The passengers had taken their seats—the one lady on the box—and Sam Rice stood, chronometer held daintily between thumb and finger, waiting for the second hand to come round the quarter of a minute, while the grooms slipped the last strap of the harness into its buckle. At the expiration of the quarter of a minute, as Sam stuck an unlighted cigar between his lips and took hold of the box to pull himself up to his seat, the good-natured landlady of Piney-woods Station called out, with some officiousness:

"Mr. Rice, don't you want a match?"

"That's just what I've been looking for these ten years," responded Sam, and at that instant his eyes were on a level with the lady's on the box, so that he could not help seeing the roguish glint of them, which so far disconcerted the usually self-possessed professor of the whip that he heard not the landlady's laugh, but gathered up the reins in such a hasty and careless manner as to cause Demon, the nighleader, to go off with a bound that nearly threw the owner of the eyes out of her place. The little flurry gave opportunity for Mrs. Dolly Page—that was the lady's name—to drop her veil over her face, and for Sam Rice to show his genteel handling of the ribbons and conquer the unaccountable disturbance of his pulses.

Sam had looked at the waybill not ten minutes before to ascertain the name of the pretty black-eyed woman seated at his left hand, and the consciousness of so great a curiosity gratified may have augmented his unaccustomed embarrassment. Certain it is, Sam Rice had driven six horses on a ticklish mountain road for four years without missing a trip, and had more than once encountered the "road agents" without ever yet delivering them an express box, had had old and young ladies, plain and beautiful ones, to sit beside him hundreds of times, yet this was the first time he had consulted the waybill on his own account to find a lady's name. This one time, too, it had a *Mrs.* before it, which prefix gave him a pang he was very unwilling to own. On the other hand, Mrs. Dolly Page was clad in extremely deep black. Could she be in mourning for Mr. Page? If Demon had an unusual number of starting fits that afternoon, his driver was not altogether guiltless in the matter, for what horse, so sensitive as he, would not have felt the magnetism of something wrong behind him?

But as the mocking eyes kept hidden behind a veil, and the rich musical voice uttered not a word through a whole half hour, which seemed an age to Sam, he finally recovered himself so far as to say he believed he would not smoke, after all, and thereupon returned the cigar, still unlighted, to his pocket.

"I hope you do not deprive yourself of a luxury on my account," murmured the soft voice.

"I guess this dust and sunshine is enough for a lady to stand, without my smokin' in her face," returned Sam, politely, and glancing at the veil.

"Still, I beg you will smoke, if you are accustomed," persisted the cooing voice behind it. But Sam, to his praise be it spoken, refused to add anything to the discomforts of a summer day's ride across the mountains. His chivalry had its reward, for the lady thus favored, feeling constrained to make some return for such consideration, began to talk, in a vein that delighted her auditor, about horses—their points and their traits—and, lastly, about their drivers.

"I have always fancied," said Mrs. Dolly Page, "that if I were a man, I should take to stage-driving as a profession. It seems to me a free and manly calling, one that develops some of the best qualities of a man. Of course, it has its drawbacks. One cannot always choose one's society on a stage, and there are temptations to bad habits. Besides, there are storms and upsets and all that sort of thing. I've often thought," continued Mrs. Dolly, "that we do not consider enough the hardships of drivers, nor what we owe them. You've read that poem—the 'Postboy's Song':
'Like a shuttle thrown by the hand of Fate,
Forward and back I go.'

"Well, it is just so. They do bring us our letters, full of good and ill news, helping to weave the web of Fate for us, yet not to blame for what tidings they bring, and always faithful to their duties, in storm or shine."

"I shall like my profession better after what you have said of it," answered Sam, giving his whip a curl to make it touch the off-leader's right ear. "I've done my duty mostly, and not complained of the hardships, though once or twice I've been too beat out to get off the box at the end of my drive, but that was in a long spell of bad weather when the roads was just awful and the rain as cold as snow."

"Would you mind letting me hold the lines awhile?" asked the cooing voice, at last. "I've driven a six-in-hand before."

Though decidedly startled and averse to trusting his team to such a pair of hands, Sam was compelled, by the psychic force of the little woman, to yield up the reins. It was with fear and trembling that he watched her handling of them for the first mile, but, as she really seemed to know what she was about, his confidence increased, and he watched her with admiration. Her veil was now up, her eyes were sparkling, and cheeks glowing. She did not speak often, but, when she did, it was always something piquant and graceful that she uttered. At last, just as the station was in sight, she yielded up the lines, with a deep-drawn sigh of satisfaction, apologizing for it by saying that her hands, not being used to it, were tired. "I'm not sure," she added, "but I shall take to the box, at last, as a steady thing."

"If you do," responded Sam, gallantly, "I hope you will drive on my line."

"Thanks. I shall ask you for a reference when I apply for the situation."

There was then a halt, a supply of fresh horses, and a prompt, lively start. But the afternoon was intensely hot, and the team soon sobered down. Mrs. Page did not offer again to take the lines. She was overwarm and weary, perhaps, quiet and a little sad, at any rate. Mr. Rice was quiet, too, and thoughtful. The passengers inside were asleep. The coach rattled along at a steady pace, with the dust so deep under the wheels as to still their rumble. At intervals, a freight-wagon was passed, drawn to one side at a "turnout," or a rabbit skipped across the road, or a solitary horseman suggested alternately a "road agent," or one of James's heroes. Grand views presented themselves of wooded cliffs and wild ravines. Tall pines threw lengthening shadows across the open spaces on the mountainside. And so the afternoon wore away, and, when the sun was setting, the passengers alighted for their supper at the principal hotel of Lucky-dog—a mining-camp pretty well up in the Sierras.

"We both stop here," said Sam, as he helped the lady down from her high position, letting her know by this remark that her destination was known to him.

"I'm rather glad of that," she answered frankly, with a little smile, and, considering all that had transpired on that long drive, Sam was certainly pardonable if he felt almost sure that her reason for being glad was identical with his own.

Lucky-dog was one of those shambling, new camps where one street serves for a string on which two or three dozen ill-assorted tenements are strung, every fifth one being a place intended for the relief of the universal American thirst, though the liquids dispensed at these beneficent institutions were observed rather to provoke than to abate the dryness of their patrons. Eating houses were even more frequent than those that dispensed moisture to parched throats, so that, taking a cursory view of the windows fronting on the street, the impression was inevitably conveyed of the expected rush of famished armies, whose wants this charitable community was only too willing to supply for a sufficient consideration. The houses that were not eating and drinking houses were hotels, if we except occasional grocery and general merchandise establishments. Into what out-of-the-way corners the inhabitants were stowed, it was impossible to conjecture, until it was discovered that the men lived at the places already inventoried and that women abode not at all in Lucky-dog—or if there were any, not more than a half a dozen of them, and they lived in unaccustomed places.

The advent of Mrs. Page at the Silver Brick Hotel naturally made a sensation. An assemblage of not less than fifty gentlemen of leisure crowded about the entrance, each more intent than the other on getting a look at the arrivals, and especially at this one arrival—whose age, looks, name, business, and intentions in coming to Lucky-dog were discussed with great freedom. Sam Rice was closely questioned but proved reticent and noncommittal. The landlord was besieged with inquiries—the landlady, too—and all without anybody being made much the wiser. There was the waybill, and there was the lady herself; put that and that together, and make what you could of it.

Mrs. Dolly Page did not seem discomposed in the least by the evident interest she inspired. With her black curls smoothly brushed, her black robes immaculately neat, with a pretty color in her round cheeks, and a quietly absorbed expression in her whole bearing, she endured the concentrated gaze of fifty pairs of eyes during the whole of dinner, without so much as one awkward movement or the dropping of a fork or teaspoon. So it was plain that the curious would be compelled to await Mrs. Page's own time for developments.

But developments did not seem likely to come overwhelmingly. Mrs. Page made a fast friend of the landlady of the Silver Brick, by means of little household arts peculiarly her own, and, before a fortnight was gone, had become as indispensable to all the boarders as she was to Mrs. Shaughnessy herself. If she had a history, she kept it carefully from curious ears. Mrs. Shaughnessy was evidently satisfied and challenged criticism of her favorite. Indeed, there was nothing to criticise. It was generally understood that she was a widow who had to get on in the world as best she could, and thus the public sympathy was secured, and an embargo laid upon gossip. To be sure, there were certain men in Lucky-dog, of a class which has its representatives everywhere, who regarded all unappropriated women, especially pretty women, very much as the hunter regards game, and the more difficult the approach, the more exciting the chase. But these moral Nimrods had not half the chance with self-possessed Mrs. Dolly Page than they would have had with a different style of woman. The grosser sort got a sudden *congé*, and with the more refined sportsmen she coquetted just enough to show them that two could play at a game of "make-believe" and then sent them off with a lofty scorn edifying to behold—to the mingled admiration and amusement of Mrs. Shaughnessy.

The only affair which seemed to have a kernel of seriousness in it was that of Mr. Samuel Rice. Regularly, when the stage was in, on Sam's night, he paid his respects to Mrs. Page. And Mrs. Page always received him with a graceful friendliness, asking after the horses and even sometimes going so far as to accompany him to their stables. On these occasions she never failed to carry several lumps of sugar in her pocket, which she fed to the handsome brutes off her own pink palm, until there was not one of them she could not handle at her will.

Thus passed many weeks, until summer was drawing to a close. Two or three times she had gone down to Piney-woods Station and back on Sam's coach, and always sat on the box and drove a part of the way, but never where her driving would excite remark. It is superfluous to state that on these occasions there was a happy heart beneath Sam's linen-duster, or that the bantering remarks of his brother-drivers were borne with smiling equanimity, not to say pride, for Sam was well aware that Mrs. Dolly Page's brunette beauty and his blonde-bearded style together furnished a not unpleasing *tableau* of personal charms. Besides, Sam's motto was "Let those laugh who win," and he seemed to himself to be on the road to heights of happiness beyond the ken of ordinary mortals— especially ordinary stage-drivers.

"I don't calkelate to drive stage more than a year or two longer," Sam said to Mrs. Page, confidentially, on the return from their last trip together to Piney-woods Station. "I've got a little place down in Amador and an interest in the Nip-and-tuck gold mine, besides a few hundreds in bank. I've a notion to settle down some day in a cottage with vines over the porch, with a little woman to tend the flowers in the front garden."

As if Sam's heightened color and shining eyes had not sufficiently pointed this confession of his desires, it chanced that at this moment the eyes of both were attracted to a wayside picture: a cottage, a flower-bordered walk, a fair young woman standing at the gate, with a crowing babe in her arms lifting its little white hands to the sun-browned face of a stalwart young farmer who was smiling proudly on the two. At this sudden apparition of his inmost thoughts, Sam's heart gave a great bound, and there was a simultaneous ringing in his ears. His first instinctive act was to crack his whip so fiercely as to set the leaders off prancing, and when, by this diversion, he had partly recovered self-possession to glance at the face of his companion, a new embarrassment seized him when he discovered two little rivers of tears running over the crimsoned cheeks. But a coach-box is not a convenient place for sentiment to display itself, and, though the temptation was great to inquire into the cause of the tears, with a view of offering consolation, Sam prudently looked the other way and maintained silence. The reader, however, knows that those tears sank into the beholder's soul and caused to germinate countless tender thoughts and emotions, which were, on some future occasion, to be laid upon the altar of his devotion to Mrs. Dolly Page. And nonetheless, that, in a few minutes, the eyes which shed them resumed their roguish brightness, and the lady was totally unconscious of having heard, seen, or felt any embarrassment. Sentiment between them was successfully *tabooed,* so far as utterance was concerned, for that time. And so Sam found, somewhat to his disappointment, it continued to fall out, that whenever he got upon delicate ground, the lady was off like a hummingbird, darting hither and yon, so that it was impossible to put a finger upon her or get so much as a look at her brilliant and restless wings. But nobody ever tired of trying to find a hummingbird at rest, and so Sam never gave up looking for the opportune moment of speaking his mind.

Meanwhile, Lucky-dog Camp was having a fresh sensation. An organized band of gamblers, robbers, and "road agents" had made a swoop upon its property, of various kinds, and had succeeded in making off with it. The very night after the ride just mentioned, the best horses in Sam Rice's team were stolen, making it necessary to substitute what Sam called "a pa'r of ornery cayuses." To put the climax to his misfortunes, the "road agents" attacked him next morning when, the "ornery cayuses" becoming unmanageable, Sam was forced to surrender the treasure box, and the passengers their bullion. The excitement in Lucky-dog was intense. A vigilance committee, secretly organized, lay in waiting for the offenders and, after a week or two, made a capture of a well-known sporting man whose presence in camp had for some time been regarded with suspicion. Short shrift was afforded him. That same afternoon his gentlemanly person swung dangling from a gnarled pine-tree limb, and his frightened soul had fled into outer darkness.

When this event became known to Mrs. Dolly Page, she turned ghostly white and then fainted dead away. Mrs. Shaughnessy was very much concerned for her friend, berating in round terms the brutishness of people who could talk of such things before a tender-hearted lady like that. To Mr. Rice, particularly, she expatiated upon the coarseness of certain people and the refined sensitiveness of others, and Sam was much inclined to agree with her, so far as her remarks applied to her friend, who was not yet recovered sufficiently to be visible. Indeed, Mrs. Page was not visible for so many days that Sam's soul began to long for her with a mighty longing. At length, she made her appearance, considerably paler and thinner than was her wont, but doubly interesting and lovely to the eyes of so partial an observer as Sam, who would willingly have sheltered her weakness in his strong, manly arms. Sam, naturally enough, would never have hinted at the event which had so distressed her, but she relieved him of all embarrassment on that subject by saying to him almost at once: "Mr. Rice, I am told they have not buried the man they hung, so shockingly, the other day. They certainly will not leave him *there?*" she added, with a shudder.

"I don't know—I suppose," stammered Sam, "it is their way, with them fellows."

"But you will not allow it? You cannot allow it!" she said excitedly.

"I couldn't prevent them," said Sam, quite humbly.

"Mr. Rice," and her voice was at once a command and an entreaty, "you *can* and *must* prevent it. You are not afraid? I will go with you—this very night—and will help you. Don't say you will not, for I cannot sleep until it is done. I have not slept for a week."

She looked so white and so wild as she uttered this confession that Sam would have been the wretch he was not, to refuse her. So he said, "Don't you fret. I'll bury him, if it troubles you so. But you needn't go along. You couldn't; it's too far, and you're too weak," seeing how she trembled.

"I am not weak—only nervous. I prefer to go along. But we must be secret, I suppose? Oh!" she said with a start that was indeed "nervous."

"Yes, we must be secret," said Sam, and he looked as if he did not half like the business but would not refuse.

"You are a good man, Mr. Rice, and I thank you." And with that, Mrs. Dolly Page caught up one of his hands and, kissing it hastily, began to cry as she walked quickly away.

"Don't cry, and don't go until I have promised to do whatever you ask, if it will make you well again," Sam said, following her to the door.

"Then call for me to take a walk with you tonight. The moon is full, but no one will observe us. They would not think of our going *there*," she said with another shudder—and she slipped away from his detaining hand.

That evening Mr. Samuel Rice and Mrs. Page took a walk by moonlight. Laughing gossips commented on it after their fashion, and disagreeable gossips remarked that they came home very late, after *their* fashion. But nobody, they believed, saw where they went, or what they did. Yet those two came from performing an act of

Christian charity, each with a sense of guilt and unworthiness very irritating to endure, albeit from very different causes. One, because an unwelcome suspicion had thrust itself into his mind, and the other—

The ground of Sam's suspicion was a photograph, which, in handling the gambler's body somewhat awkwardly, by reason of its weight—Mrs. Page had found, at the last, she could not render any assistance—had slipped from some receptacle in its clothing. A hasty glance, under the full light of the moon, had shown him the features of the lady who sat twelve paces away with her hands over her face. It is not always those who sin who suffer most from the consciousness of sin, and Sam, perhaps, with that hint of possible—nay, almost certain—wickedness in his breast pocket, was more burdened by the weight of it than many a criminal about to suffer all the terrors of the law, for the woman who he loved stood accused, if not convicted, before his conscience and her own, and he could not condemn, because his heart refused to judge her.

When the two stood together under the light of the lamp in the deserted parlor of the Silver Brick Hotel, the long silence that, by her quick perceptions, had been recognized as accusing her, upon what evidence she did not yet know, was at length broken by Sam's voice, husky with agitation.

"Mrs. Page," he said, assuming an unconscious dignity of mien and sternness of countenance, "I shall ask you some questions, sometime, which you may not think quite polite. And you must answer me, you understand. I'm bound to know the truth about this man."

"About this man!" Then he suspected her of connection with the wretched criminal whose body had only just now been hidden from mocking eyes? How much did he suspect? How much did he *know?* Her pale face and frightened eyes seemed to ask these questions of him, but not a sound escaped her lips. The imploring look, so strange upon her usually bright face, touched all that was tender in Sam's romantic nature. In another moment he would have recalled his demand and trusted her infinitely, but in that critical moment she fainted quite away, to his mingled sorrow and alarm, and Mrs. Shaughnessy being summoned, Sam received a wordy reprimand for having no more sense than to keep a sick woman up half of the night; smarting under which undeserved censure, he retired to think over the events of the evening.

The hour of departure from Lucky-dog, for Sam's coach, was four o'clock in the morning, and its driver was not a little surprised, when about to mount the box, to discover Mrs. Page waiting to take a seat beside him. After the adventure of the previous night, it was with some restraint that he addressed her, and there was wanting, also, something of his cheerful alacrity of manner when he requested the stranger who had taken the box seat to yield it to a lady. The stranger's mood seemed uncongenial, for he declined to abdicate, intimating that there was room for the lady between himself and the driver, if she insisted upon an outside seat.

But Mrs. Page did not insist. She whispered Sam to open the coach door and quietly took a seat inside, and Sam, with a sense of irritation very unusual with him, climbed reluctantly to his place, giving the "cayuses" the lash in a way that set them off on a keen run. By the time he had gotten his team cooled down, the unusual mood had passed, and the longing returned to hear the sweet voice and watch the bright eyes that had made his happiness on former occasions. Puzzled as he was and pained by the evidence he possessed of her connection, in some way, with the victim of lynch law, *that* seemed like a dream in the clear, sunny air of morning, while the more blissful past asserted its claim to be considered reality. Not a lark, warbling its flute-notes by the wayside, not a pretty bit of the familiar landscape, nor glimpse of brook that leaped sparkling down the mountain, but recalled some charming utterance of Mrs. Dolly Page, as he first knew her, as he could not now recognize her in the pale, nervous, and evidently suffering woman sitting, closely veiled, inside the coach.

Occupied with these thoughts, Sam felt a disagreeable shock when the outside passenger—in a voice that contrasted roughly with that other voice which was murmuring in his ear—began a remark about the mining prospects of Lucky-dog.

"Some rich discoveries made in the neighborhood, eh? Did you ever try your luck at mining?"

"Waal, no. I own a little stock, though," answered Sam, carelessly.

"In what mine?"

"In the Nip-and-tuck."

"Good mine, from all I hear about it. Never did any prospecting?" asked the stranger, in that tone which denotes only a desire to make talk, with a view to kill time.

"No," in the same tone.

"That's odd," stuffing a handful of cut tobacco into his mouth. "I'd have sworn 'twas you I saw swinging a pick in the cañon east of camp last night."

"I'm not much on picks," Sam returned, with a slowness that well counterfeited indifference. "I was visiting a lady last evening, which is a kind of prospecting more in my line."

"Yes, I understand; that lady inside the coach. She's a game one."

"It strikes me you're devilishly free in your remarks," said Sam, becoming irritated again.

"No offense meant, I'm sure. Take a cigar? We may as well talk this matter over calmly, Mr. Rice. You see it's ten-to-one that you are implicated in this business. Been very attentive to Mrs. Page. Made several trips together. Let her handle your horses, so she could take them out of the stable for them thieves. Buried her thieving, gambling husband for her. You see the case *looks* bad, anyway, though I'm inclined to think you've just been made a tool of. I know she's a smart one. Tain't often you find one smarter."

Sam's eyes scintillated. He was strangely minded to pitch the outside passenger off the coach. The struggle in his breast between conviction and resistance to conviction amounted to agony. He could not, in that supreme moment, discriminate between the anger he felt at being falsely accused and the grief and rage of being so horribly disillusioned. Their combined anguish paled his cheeks and set his teeth on edge, of all of which the outside passenger was coolly cognizant. As they were, at that moment, in sight of the first station, he resumed.

"Let her get up here, if she wants to; I can ride inside. I don't want to be hard on her, but mind, if you breathe a word to her about my being an officer, I'll arrest you on suspicion. Let every tub stand on its own bottom. If she's guilty, you can't help her, and don't want to, either; if she's innocent, she'll come out all right, never fear. Are you on the square, now?"

"Have you got a warrant?" asked Sam, in a low tone, as he wound the lines around the break, previous to getting down.

"You bet! But I'm in no hurry to serve it. Piney-woods Station 'ill do just as well. Telegraph office there."

Mr. Rice was not in any haste this morning, being, as he said, ahead of time. He invited Mrs. Page to take her usual place on the box, telling her the gentleman had concluded to go inside, and brought her a glass of water from the bar. While he was returning the glass, the passengers, including him of the outside, being busied assuaging their thirst with something stronger than water, a rattle of wheels and a clatter of hoofs was heard, and, lo! Mrs. Dolly Page was discovered to be practicing her favorite accomplishment of driving six-in-hand!

When the "outside" recovered from his momentary surprise, he clapped his hand on the shoulder of Mr. Rice and said, in a voice savage with spite and disappointment, "I arrest you, sir."

"Arrest and be d—d!" returned Sam. "If you had done your duty, you'd have arrested *her* while you had the chance."

"That's so. Your head is level, and if you'll assist me in getting on to Piney-woods Station in time to catch the runaway—for she can't very well drive beyond that station—I'll let you off."

"You'll wait till I'm on, I reckon. My horses can't go on that errand, and you darsn't take the up-driver's team. Put that in your pipe and smoke it, old smarty!" And Sam's eyes emitted steel-blue lightnings, though his face wore a fixed expression of smiling.

Upon inquiry, it was ascertained that horses might be procured a mile back from the station, and while the baffled officer and such of the passengers as could not wait until next day went in pursuit of them, Sam mounted one of the "cayuses" and made what haste he could after the coach and Wells, Fargo & Company's express-box. Within a mile or less of Piney-woods Station, he met the keeper, the grooms, and an odd man or two that chanced to have been about the place, all armed to the teeth, who, when they saw him, halted in surprise.

"Why, we reckoned you was dead," said the head man, with an air of disappointment.

"Dead?" repeated Sam. "Have you seen my coach?"

"That's all right, down to the station, and the plucky gal that druv it told us all about the raid the 'road agents' made on you. Whar's the passengers? Any of 'em killed?"

"Passengers are all right. Where is Mrs. Page?"

"She cried, an' tuk on awful about ye, an' borrered a hoss to ride right on down the road to meet the other stage an' let 'em know what's up."

"She did, did she?" said Sam, very thoughtfully. "Waal, that *is* odd. Why, she ran away with my team—that's what she did, and it's all a hoax about the 'road agents.' The passengers are back at the other station."

Sam had suddenly become "all things to all men," to a degree that surprised himself. He was wrong about the horse, too, as was proven by its return to its owner four days after. By the same hand came the following letter to Mr. Samuel Rice:

> Dear Mr. Rice: It was so good of you! I thank you more than I can say. I wish I could set myself right in your eyes, for I prize your friendship dearly—dearly, but I know that I cannot. It has not been all my fault. I was married to a bad, bad man when I was only fifteen. He has ruined my life, but now he is dead, and I need not fear him. I will hereafter live as a good woman should live. The tears run down my cheeks as I write you this farewell—as they did that day when I saw that sweet woman and her babe at the farmhouse gate and knew what was in your thought. Heaven send you such a wife. Good-bye, dear Mr. Rice, good-bye.
>
> Dolly Page

There are some men, as well as women, in this world, who could figure in the role of *Evangeline,* who have tender, loyal, and constant hearts. Such a one was the driver of the Lucky-dog stage. But, though he sat on that box for two years longer and scrutinized every dark-eyed, sweet-voiced lady-passenger who rode in his coach during that time, often with an intense longing for a sight of the face he craved—it never came. Out of the heaven of his life that star had vanished forever, and nothing was left him but a soiled photograph and a tear-stained letter, worn with frequent folding and unfolding.

Miss Jorgensen

I am a plain, elderly, unmarried man, and I board at Mrs. Mason's. A great deal of what I am about to relate came under my own observation, and the remainder was confided to me from time to time by my landlady, with whom I am upon terms of friendship and intimacy, having had a home in her house for a period of seven years.

Mrs. Mason lives in her own tenement in a quiet part of the city and, besides myself, has usually three or four other boarders, generally teachers or poor young authors—some person always of the class that, having few other pleasures, makes it a point to secure rooms with a fine view of the bay. When Miss Jorgensen came to us, we were a quiet, studious, yet harmonious and happy family; so well satisfied with our little community that we did not take kindly to the proposed addition to our circle when Mrs. Mason mentioned it. Neither did our landlady seem to desire any change, but she explained to us that the young person applying had made a strong appeal, that her classes (she was a teacher of French) were principally in our part of the city, and that she would be satisfied with a mere closet for a room. The only privilege for which she stipulated was the use of the common parlor twice a week to receive her company in.

"But I cannot agree to give up the parlor any single evening," Mrs. Mason replied, "because it is used by all the family, every evening. You will be entitled to the same privileges with the others." After some hesitation this was agreed to, and our new boarder was installed in the upper hall bedroom, which, when it had received the necessary furniture and a Saratoga trunk, with numerous boxes and baskets, would scarcely allow space enough to dress in. However, Mrs. Mason reported that the tenant professed real satisfaction with her quarters, and we all were on tiptoe with curiosity to see the new inmate.

"Miss Jorgensen," said Mrs. Mason that evening, as she escorted to the dinner table a small, pale, dark-eyed young person in deep mourning, and we being severally and separately presented afterward, endeavored to place this little lonely scrap of humanity at ease with ourselves. But in this well-intentioned effort Miss Jorgensen did not seem to meet us halfway. On the contrary, she repelled us. She was reserved without being diffident, mercilessly critical, and fierily disputatious—all of which we found out in less than a week. She never entered or left a room without somehow disturbing the mental atmosphere of it and giving the inmates a little shock, so that Mr. Quivey, our dramatic writer, soon took to calling her the "Electrical Eel," substituting "E.E." when the person indicated was within earshot possibly or probably. In return, as we afterward discovered, Miss Jorgensen told Miss Flower, our other young lady boarder, that she had christened Mr. Quivey "I.I."—"Incurable Idiot." How the "E.E." came to her knowledge was never made plain. Before three months were past, she had quarreled with everyone in the house except Mrs. Mason and myself; though, to her credit be it said, she always apologized for her tempers when they were over, with a frankness that disarmed resentment. Nevertheless, she was so frequently in a hostile attitude toward one or another in the family that the mere mention of Miss Jorgensen's name was sure to arrest attention and excite expectations. Thus, when I only chanced to whisper to Mrs. Mason at breakfast one morning, "Miss Jorgensen keeps late hours," everyone at the table glanced our way inquiringly, as much as to ask, "What has the little woman done now?" And when she appeared at the close of the meal with pale face and swollen eyes, explaining her tardiness by saying she had a headache, no one gave her sympathizing looks except the landlady.

That kindhearted person confided to me, later in the day, that her new boarder troubled and puzzled her very much. "She will sit up until one or two o'clock every night, writing something or other, and that makes her late to breakfast. She goes out teaching every morning and comes back tired and late to luncheon, and you see she is never in her place at dinner until the soup is removed and everyone at the table helped. When I once suggested that she ought not to sit up so long at night and that her classes should be arranged not to fatigue her so much, with other bits of friendly advice, she gave me to understand, very promptly, that her ways were her own and not to be interfered with by anyone. And directly afterward the tears came into her eyes. I confess I did not understand her at all."

"What about the young man who calls here twice a week?" I inquired.

"She is engaged to him, she says."

"What sort of a person does he seem to be?"

"He looks well enough, only rather shabby, is very quiet, very attentive to her, and what you might call obedient to her requirements. She often seems displeased with him, but what she says to him at such times is unknown to me, for she does her scolding all in French, and he usually then invites her out to walk, by way of diversion, I suppose."

"Do you know that he comes every morning and carries her books for her? He certainly cannot be employed, or he would not have time for such gallantries."

"Perhaps he is engaged on one of the morning papers and so is off duty in the forenoon. I cannot think so industrious a person as she would take up with a man both poor and idle. But you never know what a woman will do," sighed Mrs. Mason, who had known something of heart troubles in her youth and could sympathize with other unlucky women. "Excuse me, I must not stand here gossiping." And the good lady went about her house affairs.

A few moments later I was hurrying downtown to my office when I overtook Miss Jorgensen and Mr. Hurst. As usual, she was leaning upon his arm, and he was carrying her books. She was talking excitedly, in French, and I thought her to be crying, though her face was covered with a black veil. The few words I caught before she recognized me reminded me of my conversation with Mrs. Mason.

"You *must* get something to do, Harry," she was saying. "You know that I work every instant of the time, yet how little I can save if I have to supply you with money. It is a shame to be so idle and helpless when there is so much to be done before—"

She perceived me and stopped short. "So," I thought, "this precious scamp is living off the earnings of the little French teacher, is he? A pretty fellow, truly! I'll get him his *congé* if I have to make love to her myself." Which latter conceit so amused me that I had forgotten to be indignant with Mr. Hurst before I reached my office and plunged into the business of the day.

But I never made love to Miss Jorgensen. She was not the kind of person even a flirtish man would choose to talk sentiment with, and I was always far enough from being a gallant. So our affairs went on in just the usual way at Mrs. Mason's for three or four months. Miss Jorgensen and Mr. Quivey let fly their arrows of satire at each other; Miss Flower, the assistant high-school teacher, enacted the amiable go-between; our "promising young artist" was wisely neutral; Mrs. Mason and myself were presumed to be old enough to be out of the reach of boardinghouse tiffs and preserved a prudent unconsciousness. Mr. Hurst continued to call twice a week in the evening, and Miss Jorgensen kept on giving French lessons by day and writing out translations for the press at night. She was growing very thin, very pale, and cried a good deal, as I had reason to know, for her room adjoined mine, and more than a few times I had listened to her sobbing, until I felt almost forced to interfere, but interfered I never had yet.

One foggy July evening, on coming home to dinner, I encountered Miss Jorgensen in the hall. She appeared to be just going out, a circumstance which surprised me somewhat on account of the hour. I, however, opened the door for her without comment when, by the fading daylight, I perceived that her face was deathly pale and her black eyes burning. She passed me without remark and hurried off into the foggy twilight. Nor did she appear at dinner, but came in about eight o'clock and went directly to her own room. When Mrs. Mason knocked at her door to inquire if she was not going to take some refreshments, the only reply that could be elicited was that she had a headache and could not be induced to eat or drink—spoken through the closed door.

"She's been having a row with that sunflower of hers," was Mr. Quivey's comment when he overheard Mrs. Mason's report to me, made in an undertone. Truth to tell, Mr. Quivey, from associating so much with theatrical people in the capacity of playwright, had come to be rather stagy in his style at times. "By the way, he was not on escort duty this morning. I saw her proceeding along Powell Street alone and anxiously peering up and down all the cross streets, evidently on the lookout, but he failed to put in an appearance."

"Which was very unkind of him, if she expected that he would," put in Miss Flower, glancing from under her long lashes at the speaker.

"That is so," returned Quivey, "for the fellow does nothing else, I do believe, but play lackey to Miss Jorgensen, and if that is his sole occupation, he ought to perform that duty faithfully. I do not see, for my part, how he pays his way."

"Perhaps it pays him to be a lackey," I suggested, remembering what I had once overheard between them. Mrs. Mason gave me a cautioning glance, which she need not have done, for I had no intention of making known Miss Jorgensen's secrets.

"Well," said Miss Flower, as if she had been debating the question in her mind for some time previous, "I doubt if a woman can love a man who submits to her will as subserviently as Mr. Hurst seems to, to Miss Jorgensen. I know *some women* could not."

"By which you mean *you* could not," Mrs. Mason returned, smiling. "I do not see that the case need be very different with men. Subserviency never won anybody's respect or love either. Neither does willful opposition anymore. Proper self-respect and a fair share of self-love is more sure of winning admiration, from men or women, than too little self-assertion or too much."

"But where the self-assertion is all on one side and the self-abasement all on the other—as in the case of Miss Jorgensen and Mr. Hurst—then how would you establish an equilibrium, Mrs. Mason?"

"It establishes itself in that case, I should say," clipped in Mr. Quivey. "Oil and water do not mix, but each keeps its own place perfectly and without disturbance."

I do not know how long this conversation might have gone on in this half-earnest, half-facetious style, with Miss Jorgensen for its object, had not something happened just here to bring it abruptly to a close, and that something was the report of a pistol over our very heads.

"Great heaven!" ejaculated Miss Flower, losing all her color and self-possession together.

"E.E., as I live—she has shot herself!" cried Quivey, half-doubting, half-convinced.

I caught these words as I made a rapid movement toward the staircase. They struck me as so undeniably true that I never hesitated in making an assault upon her door.

It was locked on the inside, and I could hear nothing except a faint moaning sound within. Fearing the worst, I threw my whole weight and strength against it, and it flew open with a crash. There lay Miss Jorgensen upon the floor, in the middle of her little room, uttering low moaning sobs, though apparently not unconscious. I stooped over and lifted her in my arms to lay her upon the bed, and as I did so, a small pocket pistol fell at my feet, and I discovered blood upon the carpet.

"Yes, Miss Jorgensen had certainly shot herself," I told Mrs. Mason and the rest who crowded after us into the little woman's room, but whether dangerously or not, I could not say, nor whether purposely or accidentally. Probably not dangerously, as she was already making signs to me to exclude people from the apartment.

"You had better bring a surgeon," I said to Quivey, who turned away muttering, followed by Miss Flower.

With Mrs. Mason's assistance, I soon made out the location of the wound, which was in the flesh of the upper part of the left arm, and consequently not so alarming as it would be painful during treatment.

"Could she have meant to shoot herself through the heart, and failed through agitation?" whispered Mrs. Mason to me, aside.

"No, no, it was an accident," murmured the victim, whose quick ear had caught the words. "I did not mean to shoot myself."

"Poor child, I am very sorry for you," returned Mrs. Mason gently, whose kind heart had always leaned toward the little French teacher, in spite of her singular ways. "It is very unfortunate, but you shall receive careful nursing until you recover. You need not worry about yourself, but try to bear it the best you can."

"O, I cannot bear it—I *must* be well tomorrow. O, what shall I do?" moaned Miss Jorgensen. "O, that this should have happened tonight!" And momently, after this thought occurred to her, her restlessness seemed to increase, until the surgeon came and began an examination of the wound.

While this was going on, notwithstanding the sickening pain, the sufferer seemed anxious only about the opinion to be given upon the importance of the wound as interfering with her usual pursuits.

When, in answer to a direct appeal, she was told that it must be some weeks before she could resume going out, a fainting fit immediately followed, which gave us no little trouble and alarm.

Before taking leave, the doctor accompanied me to my own apartment and proceeded to question me.

"What is the history of the case?" said he. "Is there anything peculiar in the life or habits of Miss Jorgensen to account for her great anxiety to get well immediately?"

"She fears to lose her classes, I presume, and there may be other engagements which are unknown to us." I still had a great reluctance to saying what I suspected might be troubling Miss Jorgensen.

"Neither of which accounts for all that I observe in her case," returned the doctor. "What are her connections—has she any family ties—any lover, even?"

"I believe she told Mrs. Mason she was engaged to a young man who calls here twice a week."

"Ah! Do you know where this young man is to be found? It might be best to communicate with him in the morning. Possibly he may be able to dispel this anxious fear of hers, from whatever cause it arises."

I promised the doctor to speak to Mrs. Mason about it, and he soon after took leave, having first satisfied himself that the unlucky pistol was incapable of doing further mischief and was safely hidden from Miss Jorgensen.

Naturally, the next morning, the table talk turned upon the incident of the evening previous.

"She need not tell me that it was an accident," Mr. Quivey was saying, very decidedly. "She is just the sort of woman for desperate remedies, and she is tired of living, with that vampire friend of hers draining her lifeblood!"

I confess I felt startled by the correspondence of Quivey's opinion with my own, for I had heretofore believed that myself and Mrs. Mason were the only persons who suspected that Hurst was dependent upon Miss Jorgensen for the means of living. In my surprise I said, "You know that he does this?"

"I know that Craycroft paid him yesterday for a long translation done by Miss Jorgensen, and I do not believe he had an order for it, other than verbal. Craycroft, seeing them so much together, paid the money and took a receipt."

"Perhaps he paid the money to Mr. Hurst by her instructions, for her own use," suggested Miss Flower. "But then he did not see her last evening, did he? I hope he does not rob Miss Jorgensen. Such a delicate little woman has enough to do to look out for herself, I should think."

"One thing is certain," interposed Mrs. Mason, "Miss Jorgensen does what she does, and permits what she permits, intelligently, and our speculations concerning her affairs will not produce a remedy for what we fancy we see wrong in them." Which hint had the effect of silencing the discussion for that time.

Before I left the house that morning, I had a consultation with Mrs. Mason, who had passed the night in attendance upon Miss Jorgensen and who had informed me that she had been very restless, in spite of the quieting prescription left by the doctor. "I wish you would go up and speak to her," Mrs. Mason said. "Perhaps you can do something for her which I could not, and I am sure she needs some such service."

Thus urged, I obeyed an impulse of my own, which had been to do this very thing. When I tapped softly at her door, she said, "Come in!" in a pained and petulant tone, as if any interruption was wearisome to her, but when she saw who it was, her countenance assumed an eager and animated expression, which rewarded me at once for the effort I was making.

"Thank you for coming to see me," said she quickly. "I was almost on the point of sending for you." Pausing for a moment, while her eyes searched my face, she continued, "I am in trouble, which cannot be all explained, and which will force you, if you do a service for me, to take me very much upon trust, but I will first assure you that what you may do for me will not involve *you* in any difficulty. More than this I cannot now say. Will you do this service for me and keep your agency in the matter secret? The service is slight, the importance of secrecy great."

I expressed my willingness to do anything which would not compromise me with myself and that, I told her, I did not fear her requiring.

She then proceeded, with some embarrassment, to say that she wished a note conveyed to Mr. Hurst, upon which I smiled, and answered, "I had conjectured as much."

"But you must not conjecture anything," she replied, with some asperity, "for you are sure to go wide of the truth. You think I have only to send for Mr. Hurst to bring him here, but you are mistaken. He cannot come, because he *dare* not. He is in hiding, but I cannot tell you why. Only do not betray him; I ask no more. You are not called upon to do any more—to do anything against him, I mean." Seeing me hesitate, she continued, "I need not tell you that I believe my life is in your hands. I have been living a long time with all my faculties upon a severe strain, so severe that I feel I shall go mad if the pressure is increased. I entreat you not to refuse me."

"Very well," I answered, "I will do what you require."

"It is only to take this—" she pulled a note from beneath her pillow, addressed to 'Mr. Harry Hurst,' and handed it to me "—to the address, which you will have no difficulty in finding, though I am sorry to have to send you on a walk so out of your way. And please take this also—" handing me a roll of coin, marked $100. "No answer is expected. Of course, you will not give these things to anyone but Mr. Hurst. That is all." And she sunk back wearily upon her pillow, with closed eyes, as if she had no further interest in the affair.

I know as well as if she had told me that this note was a warning to fly, and this money the means to make flight good. I had promised to deliver them on her simple entreaty and assurance that I should not dishonor myself. But might I not wrong society? Might not she be herself deceived about Hurst? The assertion of Quivey that he had collected money from her employers the day before occurred to me. Did she know it or not? I questioned while regarding the thin, pale, weary face on the pillow before me. While I hesitated she opened her eyes with a wondering, impatient gaze.

"Do you repent?" she asked.

"I deliberate, rather," I replied. "I chanced to learn yesterday that Mr. Hurst had drawn money from Craycroft & Co. and was thinking that if you knew it, you might not wish to send this also."

For an instant her black eyes blazed with anger, but whether at me or at Mr. Hurst I could not tell, and she seemed to hesitate, as I had done.

"Yes, take it," she said, with hopeless sadness in her tone. "He may need it and, for myself, what does it matter now?"

"I shall do as you bid me," I replied, "but it is under protest, for it is my impression that you are doing yourself an injury and Mr. Hurst no good."

"You don't understand," she returned, sharply. "Now go, please."

"Very well, I am gone. But I promise you that if you exact services of me, I shall insist on your taking care of your health by way of return. You are in a fever at this moment, which I warn you will be serious if not checked. Here comes the doctor. Good morning."

I pass over the trifling incidents of my visit to the residence of Mr. Hurst. Suffice to say that Mr. Hurst had departed to parts unknown, and that I had to carry about all day Miss Jorgensen's letter and money. On returning home to dinner that afternoon, I found a stranger occupying Miss Jorgensen's place at table. He was a shrewd-looking man of about forty years, talkative, versatile, and what you might call "jolly." Nothing escaped his observation; nothing was uttered that he did not hear, often replying most unexpectedly to what was not intended for him—a practice that would have been annoying but for a certain tact and good humor which disarmed criticism. The whole family, while admitting that our new day-boarder was not exactly congenial, confessed to liking his amusing talk immensely.

"He quite brightens us up, don't you think so, Mr. Quivey?" was Miss Flower's method of endorsing him.

"He does very well just now," replied Quivey, "though I'd lots rather see E.E. back in that place. When one gets used to pickles or pepper, one wants pickles or pepper; honey palls on the appetite."

"I thought you had almost too much pepper sometimes," said Miss Flower, remembering the "I.I."

"It's a healthful stimulant," returned Quivey, ignoring the covert reminder.

"But not always an agreeable one."

I suspected that Miss Flower, who had an intense admiration for dramatic talent, entertained her own reasons for jogging Mr. Quivey's memory, and being willing to give her every opportunity to promote her own views, I took this occasion to make my report to Miss Jorgensen. As might have been expected, she had been feverishly anticipating my visit. I had no sooner entered the room than she uttered her brief interrogation:

"Well?"

I laid the note and the money upon the bed. "You see how it is?" I said.

"He is gone?"

"Yes."

"I am so very glad!" she said with emphasis, while something like a smile lighted up her countenance. "This gives me a respite, at least. If he is prudent—" She checked herself, and giving me a grateful glance, exclaimed, "I am so much obliged to you!"

"Nobody could be more welcome, I am sure, to so slight a service. I shall hope now to see you getting well."

"O, yes," she answered. "I must get well; there is so much to do. But my classes and my writing must be dropped for a while, I presume, unless the doctor will let me take in some of my scholars, for, of course, I cannot go out."

"Your arm must begin to heal before you can think of teaching, ever so little. I have an idea, Miss Jorgensen, from what you have said of yourself, that this necessity for repose, which is forced upon you, will prove to be an excellent thing. Certainly, you were wearing out very fast with your incessant labor."

"Perhaps so—I mean, perhaps enforced rest will not be bad for me, but, O, there is such need to work! I can so poorly afford to be idle."

"What you say relieves my mind of a suspicion, which at first I harbored, that the firing of that mischievous pistol was not wholly accidental. I now see you wish to live and work. But why had you such a weapon about you? Are you accustomed to firearms?"

"The mischief this one did me shows that I am not, and my having it about me came from a fear I had of its doing worse mischief in the hands of Mr. Hurst."

"Are affairs so desperate with him?"

"Please don't question me. I cannot answer you satisfactorily. Mr. Hurst is in trouble, and the least that is said or known about him is the best. And yet you wonder, no doubt, that I should interest myself about a man who is compelled to act the part of a culprit. Well, I cannot tell you why at present, and it would be a great relief to know that you thought nothing more about it."

This last she uttered rather petulantly, which warned me that this conversation was doing her no good.

"Believe, then," I said, "that I have no interest in your affairs, except the wish to promote your welfare. And I think I may venture to affirm that everybody in the house is equally at your service when you wish to command him or her."

"Thank you all, but I do not deserve your kindness; I have been so ill-tempered. The truth is I cannot afford to have friends; friends pry into one's affairs so mercilessly. Mrs. Mason tells me there is a new boarder," she said, suddenly changing the subject.

I assented and gave what I intended to be an amusing account of the newcomer's conversation and manners.

"Was there anything said about me at dinner?" she asked, with a painful consciousness of the opinion I might have of such a question.

"I do not think there was. We were all so taken up with the latest acquisition that we forgot you for the time."

"May I ask this favor of you: to keep the conversation away from me as much as possible? I am morbidly sensitive, I presume," she said, with a poor attempt at a smile, "and I cannot keep from fancying, while I lie here, what you are saying about me in the dining room or parlor."

Of course, I hastened to disavow any disposition on the part of the family to make her a subject of conversation, and even promised to discountenance any reference to her whatever, if thereby she would be made more comfortable, after which I bade her good-night, having received the assurance that my visit had relieved her mind of several apprehensions.

The more I saw and thought of Miss Jorgensen, the more she interested and puzzled me. I should have inclined to the opinion that she was a little disturbed at times in her intellect, had it not been that there was apparent so much "method in her madness"— this reflection always bringing me back at last to the conclusion that her peculiarities could all be accounted for upon the hypothesis she herself presented: too much work and some great anxiety. The spectacle of this human mite fighting the battle of life, not only for herself but for the strong man who should have been her protector, worked so upon my imagination and my sympathy that I found it difficult to keep the little woman out of my thoughts.

I kept my word to her, discountenancing, as far as I could, the discussion of her affairs, and in this effort Mrs. Mason cooperated with me, but it was practically impossible to prevent the inquiries and remarks of those of the family who were not so well informed concerning her as we were. The new boarder, also, with that quick apprehension he had of every subject, had caught enough to become interested in the patient upstairs, and daily made some inquiries concerning her condition, and, as it appeared to me— grown a little morbid, like Miss Jorgensen—was peculiarly adroit in extracting information.

Three weeks slipped away, and Miss Jorgensen had passed the most painful period of suppuration and healing in her arm, and had promised to come downstairs next day to dine with the family. Mrs. Mason had just communicated the news to us in her cheeriest tones, as if each individual was interested in it, and was proceeding to turn out our coffee when a servant brought in the letters for the house and laid them beside the tray, directly under the eye of the new boarder, who sat on the landlady's left.

"Miss Jorgensen," said he, reading the address of the topmost one. "A very peculiar handwriting." Then taking up the letter, as if to further examine the writing, I observed that he was studying the postmark as well, which, being offended at his unmannerly curiosity, I sincerely hoped was illegible. But that it was only too fatally plain will soon appear.

With an air of *hauteur* I seldom assumed, I recalled the servant and ordered the letter to be taken at once to Miss Jorgensen. Before leaving the house I was informed that Miss Jorgensen wished to speak to me.

"Mr. Hurst has done a most imprudent thing!" she exclaimed, the moment I was inside the door. "I ought to have published a 'personal,' or done something to let him know I could not go to the post office, and to account for his not hearing from me."

"He has returned to the city?"

"Yes!" She fairly ground her teeth with rage at this "stupidity," as she termed it. "He always does the very thing he ought never to have done, and leaves undone the things most important to do. Of course he cannot come here, and I cannot go to him without incurring the greatest risk. I really do not know what to do next."

Tears were now coursing down her pale cheeks—tears, it seemed, as much of anger as of sorrow.

"Let him take care of himself," I said, rather hotly. "It is not your province to care for him as you do."

She gave me an indescribable look. "What can you, what can anyone know about it? He may want money; how can he take care of himself in such circumstances without money? I sent for you to contrive some plan by which he can be communicated with. Do tell me at once what to do."

"How can I tell you when, as you say, I do not know what is required. You wish to see him, I presume?"

"How can I—O, I dislike so much to ask this of you—but *will* you take a message to him?" She asked this desperately, half-expecting me to decline, as decline I did.

"Miss Jorgensen, you are now able to ride. Shall I send a carriage for you?"

"There may be those on the lookout who would instantly suspect my purpose in going out in that way. On the contrary, nobody would suspect you."

"Still, I might be observed, which would not be pleasant, I can imagine, from what you leave me to surmise. No, Miss Jorgensen, much as I should like to serve you personally, you must excuse me from connecting myself in any way with Mr. Hurst, and if I might be allowed to offer advice, I should say that in justice to yourself, you ought to cut loose from him at once."

Miss Jorgensen covered her face with one little emaciated hand and sat silent a few seconds. "Send me the carriage," she said, "and I will go."

"You forgive me?"

"You have been very good," she said. "I ought not have required more of you. I will go at once; the sooner the better."

When I had reached the head of the stairs, I turned back again to her door.

"Once more let me counsel you to free yourself from all connection with Mr. Hurst. Why should you ruin your chances of happiness for one so undeserving, as I must think he is? Keep away from him; let him shift for himself."

"You don't know what you are talking about," she replied, with a touch of the old fierceness. "I have no chances of happiness to lose. Please go."

On my way down to the office I ordered a carriage.

What happened afterward I learned from Mrs. Mason and the evening papers. Miss Jorgensen, dressed in deep black, with her face veiled, entered the carriage, directing the driver to take her to the houses of some of her pupils. At the corner of the street, a gentleman, who proved to be our day-boarder, got upon the box with the driver and remained there while Miss Jorgensen made her calls. Finding him constantly there and becoming suspicious, she ordered the carriage home and gave directions to have it return an hour later to take her downtown for some shopping. At the time set, the carriage was in attendance and conveyed her to one of the principal stores in the city. After reentering the carriage and giving her directions, our day-boarder once more mounted the box, though unobserved by her, and was conveyed with herself to the hiding place of Mr. Hurst, contriving, by getting down before the door was opened, to elude her observation.

Another carriage, containing officers of the police, was following in the wake of this one and drew up when Miss Jorgensen had entered the house where Hurst was concealed. After waiting long enough to make it certain that the person sought was within, the officers entered to search and capture.

At the moment they entered Hurst's apartment, he was saying, with much emotion, "If I can only reach China in safety, a way will be opened for me—"

"Hush!" cried Miss Jorgensen, seeing the door opened and by whom.

"All is over!" exclaimed Hurst. "I will never be taken to prison!" And, drawing a revolver, he deliberately shot himself through the head.

Miss Jorgensen was brought back to Mrs. Mason's in a fainting condition and was ill for weeks afterward. That same evening our day-boarder called and, while settling his board with Mrs. Mason, acknowledged that he belonged to the detective police, and had for months been "working up" the case of a bank robber and forger who had escaped from one of the eastern cities and been lost to observation for a year and a half.

And we further learned in the same way, and ultimately from the lady herself, that Miss Jorgensen was a myth, and that the little French teacher was Madame—, who had suffered, and toiled, and risked everything for her unworthy husband, and who deserved rather to be congratulated than consoled upon his loss.

It is now a year since all this happened, and it is the common gossip of our boardinghouse that Mr. Quivey is devoted to the little dark-eyed widow, and although Miss Flower still refers to "E.E." and "I.I.," nobody seems to be in the least disturbed by the allusion. When I say to Quivey, "Make haste slowly, my dear fellow," he returns, "Never fear, my friend; I shall know when the time comes to speak."

An Old Fool

Part I

The annual rainfall on the lower Columbia River is upward of eighty inches—often almost ninety, and the greater amount of this fall is during the winter months, from November to March, generally the least intermittent in December. I mention this climatic fact, the better to be understood in attempting to describe a certain December afternoon in the year 186–.

It lacked but two days of Christmas, and the sun had not shone out brightly for a single hour in three weeks. On this afternoon the steady pour from the clouds was a strong reminder of the ancient deluge. Between the rain itself and the mist which always accompanies the rainfall in Oregon, the world seemed nearly blotted out. Standing on the wharf at Astoria, the noble river looked like a great gray caldron of steaming water, evaporating freely at forty-two degrees. The lofty highlands on the opposite shore had lost all shape or certain altitude. The stately forest of firs along their summits was shrouded in ever-changing masses of whitish-gray fog. Nothing could be seen of the lighthouse on the headland at the mouth of the river; nothing of Tongue Point, two miles above Astoria; and only a dim presentment of the town itself and the hills at the back of it. Even the old Astorians, used to this sort of weather and not disliking it, having little to do in the wintertime and being always braced up by sea-airs that even this freshwater flood could not divest of their tonic flavor—these old sea dogs, pilots, fishermen, and other *amphibia,* were constrained at last to give utterance to mild growls at the persistent character of the storm.

A crowd of these India-rubber clad, red-cheeked, and, alas, too often red-nosed old men of the sea had taken shelter in the Railroad Saloon—called that, apparently, because there was no railroad within hundreds of miles—and were engaged in alternate wild railings at the weather, reminiscences of other storms, and whiskey-drinking; there being an opinion current among these men that waterproof garments alone did not suffice to keep out the all-prevailing wet.

"If 'twant that we're so near the sea, with a good wide sewage of river to carry off the water, we should all be drownded; thet's my view on't," said Rumway, a bar pilot whose dripping hat rim and general shiny appearance gave point to his remark.

"You can't count on the sea to befriend you this time, Captain. Better git yer ark alongside the wharf, fur we're goin' to hev the Columbia runnin' upstream tonight, sure as you're born."

"Hullo! Is that you, Joe Chillis? What brought you to town in this kind o' weather? And what do you know about the tides— that's *my* business, I calculate."

"Mebbe it is, and mebbe a bar pilot knows more about the tides than a mountain man. But there'll be a rousin' old tide tonight and a sou'wester, to boot; you bet yer life on that!"

"I'll grant you thet a mountain man knows a heap thet other men don't. But I'll never agree thet he can tell *me* anything about *my* business. Take a drink, Joe, and then let's hear some o' your mountain yarns."

"Thankee; don't keer ef I do. I can't stop to spin yarns, tho', this evenin'. I've got to git home. It won't be easy work pullin' agin the tide an hour or two from now."

"What's your hurry?" "A story—a story!" "Let's make a night of it," "O, come, Joe, you are not wanted at home. Cabin won't run away, wife won't scold," "Stop along ov us till mornin'," were the various rather noisy and ejaculatory remarks upon Chillis's avowed intention of abandoning good and appreciative company without stopping to tell one of his ever-ready tales of Indian- and bear-fighting in the Rocky Mountains thirty years before.

"Why, you ain't goin' out again till you've shaken off the water, Joe. You're dripping like a Newfoundland," said Captain Rumway, as Chillis put down his empty glass and turned toward the door, which he had entered not five minutes before. This thoughtfulness for his comfort, however, only meant, "Stay till you've taken another drink, and then maybe you will tell us a story," and Chillis knew the bait well enough to decline it.

"Thankee, Captain. One bucketful more or less won't make no difference. I'm wet to the skin now. Thank ye all, gentlemen; I've got business to attend to this evenin'. Have any of you seen Eb Smiley this afternoon?" he said while looking back, with his hand on the doorknob. "I'd like to speak to him afore I leave, ef you can tell me whar to find him."

"You'll find him in there," answered the bartender, crooking his thumb toward a room leading out of the saloon containing a tumbled single bed and a wooden settee, besides various masculine bijouterie in the shape of boots, old and new, clean and dirty; candle and cigar ends; dusty bits of paper on a stand, the chief ornament of which was a black-looking derringer; coats, vests, fishing tackle; and cheap prints, adorning the walls in the wildest disregard of effect—except, indeed, the effect aimed at were chaos.

Into this apartment Chillis unceremoniously thrust himself through the half-open door, frowning as darkly as his fine and pleasant features would admit and muttering to himself, "Damme, I thought as much."

On the wooden settee reclined a man thirty years his junior—Chillis was over sixty, though he did not look it—sleeping the heavy, stupid sleep of intoxication. The old hunter did not stand upon ceremony nor hesitate to invade the sleeper's privacy, but marched up to the settee, his ragged old blanket-coat dripping tiny streams from every separate tatter, and proceeded at once to roughly arouse the drunken man by a prolonged and vigorous shaking.

"Wha'er want? Lemme 'lone," grumbled Smiley, only dimly conscious of what was being said or done to him.

"Get up, I say. Get up, you fool, and come along home. Your wife is needin' ye. Go home and take care of her and the boy. Come along—d'ye hear?"

But the sleeper's brain was impervious to sound or sense. He only muttered, in a drowsy whisper, "Lemme 'lone," a few times and went off into a deeper stupor than before.

"You miserable cuss," snarled Chillis, in his wrath, "be d—d to you, then! Drink yerself to death, ef you want to—the sooner the better." And with this parting adjuration and an extra shake, the old mountain man, who had drank barrels of alcohol himself with comparative immunity from harm, turned his back upon this younger degenerate victim of modern whiskey and strode out of the room and the house, without stopping to reply to the renewed entreaties of his friends to remain and "make a night of it."

Making directly for the wharf, where his boat was moored, half-filled with water, he hastily bailed it out, pushed off, and, dropping the oars into the rowlocks, bent to the work before him, for the tide was already beginning to run up, and the course he had to take brought him dead against it for the first two or three miles, after which the tide would be with him, and, if there should not be too much sea, the labor of impelling the boat would be materially lessened.

The lookout from a small boat was an ugly one at three o'clock of this rainy December afternoon. A dense, cold fog had been rolling in from the sea for the last half hour, and the wind was rising with the tide. Under the shelter of the hills at the foot of which Astoria nestled, the wind did not make itself felt, but once past "The Point" and in the exposed waters of Young's Bay, the south-westers had a fair sweep of the great river, of which the bay is only an inlet. One of these dreaded storms was preparing to make itself felt, as Chillis had predicted, and as he now saw by the way in which the mist was being blown off the face of the river, and the "whitecaps" came instead. Before he arrived off "The Point," he laid down his oars, and, taking out of his coat-pocket a saturated yellow cotton handkerchief, proceeded to tie his old soft felt hat down over his ears and otherwise make ready for a struggle with wind and water—neither of them adversaries to be trifled with, as he knew.

Not a minute too soon, either, for, just when he had resumed the oars, the boat, having drifted out of her course, was caught by a wave and a blast on its broadside, and nearly upset.

"Steady, little gal," said Chillis, bringing his boat round, head to the wind. "None o' your capers now. Thar is serious work on hand, an' I want you to behave better'n ever you did afore. It's you an' me, an' the White Rose, this time, sure," and he pressed his lips together grimly and peered out from under his bent old hat at the storm, which was driving furiously against his broad breast and into his white, anxious face, almost blinding and strangling him. His boat was a small one—too small for the seas of the lower Columbia—but it was trim and light, and steered easily. Besides, the old mountaineer was a skilled oarsman, albeit this accomplishment was not a part of the education of American hunters and trappers, as it was of the French *voyageurs*. Keeping his little craft head to the wind, he took each wave squarely on the prow, and with a powerful stroke of the oars cut through it, or sprang over it, and then made ready for the next. Meanwhile, the storm increased, the rain driving at an angle of forty-five degrees and in sheets that flapped smotheringly about him like wet blankets, and threatened to swamp his boat without assistance from the waves. It was growing colder, too, and his sodden garments were of little service to protect him from the chill that comes with a south-wester, nor was the grip of the naked hands upon the oars stimulating to the circulation of his old blood through the swollen fingers.

But old Joe Chillis had a distinct comprehension of the situation and felt himself to be master of it. He had gone over to Astoria that day, not to drink whiskey and tell stories, but to do a good turn for the "White Rose." Failing in his purpose, he was going back again, at any cost, to make up for the miscarriage of that effort. Death itself could not frighten him, for what was the Columbia in a storm to the dangers he had passed through in years of hunting and trapping in the Rocky Mountains? He had seemed to bear a charmed life then; he would believe that the charm had not deserted him.

But, O, how his old arms ached, and the storm freshening every minute, with two miles further to row, in the teeth of it. The tide was with him now, but the wind was against the tide and made an ugly sea. If he only could reach the mouth of the creek before dark. If he could? Why, he must. The tide would be up so that he could not find the entrance in the dark. He worked resolutely—worked harder than ever—but he did not accomplish so much because his strength was giving out. When he first became aware of this, he heaved a great sigh, as if his heart were broken, then pressed his lips together as before and peered through the thick gray twilight, looking for the creek's mouth while yet there was a little light.

He was now in the very worst part of the bay, where the current from Young's River was strongest, setting out toward the Columbia, and where the wind had the fairest sweep, blowing from the coast across the low Clatsop plains. Only the tide and his failing strength were opposed to these; would they enable him to hold his own? He set his teeth harder than ever, but it was all in vain, and directly the catastrophe came. His strength wavered, the boat veered round, a sudden gust and roll of water took it broadside, and over she went, keel up, more than a mile from land.

But this was not the last of Joe Chillis—not by any manner of means. He had trapped beaver too many years to mind a ducking more or less, if he only had his strength. So, when he came up, he clutched an oar that was floating past him and looked about for the boat. She was not far off—the tide was holding her, bobbing up and down like a cork. In a few minutes she was righted, and Chillis had scrambled in, losing his oar while doing it and regaining it while being nearly upset again.

It had become a matter of life and death now to keep afloat, with only one oar to fight the sea, and, though holding little from the expedient in such a gale—blowing the wrong way, besides— Chillis shouted for assistance in every lull of the tempest. To his own intense astonishment, as well as relief, his hail was answered.

"Where away?" came on the wind, the sound seeming to flap and flutter like a shred of torn sail.

"Off the creek, about a mile?" shouted Chillis, with those powerful lungs of his that had gotten much of their bellows-like proportions during a dozen years of breathing the thin air of the mountains.

"All right!" was returned on the snapping, fluttering gale. After this answer, Chillis contented himself with keeping his boat right side up and giving an occasional prolonged "Oh-whoo!" to guide his rescuers through the thickening gloom. How long it seemed, with the growing darkness, and the effort to avoid another upset! But the promised help came at last in the shape of the mail carrier's plunger, her trim little mast catching his eyes, shining white and bare out of the dusk. Directly he heard the voices of the mail carrier and another.

"Where be ye? *Who* be ye?"

"Right here, under yer bow. Joe Chillis, you bet your life!"

"Waal, come aboard here, mighty quick. Make fast. Mind your boat; don't let her strike us. Pole off—pole off, with yer oar!"

"Mind *your* oars," returned Chillis, every word spoken with a yell. "I'll mind mine."

"What was the row, out there?" asks the mail carrier, making a trumpet of his hand.

"Boat flopped over; lost an oar," answered Chillis, keeping his little craft from flying on board by main force.

"Guess I won't go over tonight," says the carrier. "'Taint safe for the mail." The wind snatched the word "mail" out of his mouth and scattered it over the water as if it had been a broken bundle of letters. "I'll go back to Skippanon," he said, the letters flying every way again.

"Couldn't get over noways, now," shouted back Chillis, glad in his heart that he could not, and that the chance, or mischance, favored his previous designs. Then he said no more, but watched his boat, warding it off carefully until they reached the mouth of the creek and got inside, with nothing worse to contend against than the insolent wind and rain.

"This is a purty stiff tide, for this time o' day. It won't take long to pull up to Skippanon, with all this water pushin' along. Goin' home tonight, Joe?"

"Yes, I'm goin' home, ef I can borrer an oar," said Chillis. "My house ain't altogether safe without me, in sech weather as this."

"Safer'n most houses, ef she don't break away from her moorin's," returned the mail carrier, laughing. "Ef I can git somebody to take my place for a week, I'm comin' up to spend it with you en' do some shootin'. Nothin' like such an establishment as yours to go huntin' in—house an' boat all in one—go where you please an' stay as long as you please."

"Find me an oar to git home with, an' you can come an' stay as long as the grub holds out."

"Waal, I can do that, I guess, when we git to the landin'. I keep an extra pair or two for emergencies. But it's gittin' awful black, Chillis, an' I don't envy you the trip up the creek. It's crooked as a string o' S's, an' full o' shoals, to boot."

"It won't be shoal tonight," remarked Chillis, and he relapsed into silence.

In a few minutes the boat's bow touched the bank. "Mind the tiller!" called out both oarsmen, savagely. But as no one minded it, and it was too dark to see what was the matter, the mail carrier dropped his oar and stepped back to the stern to *feel* what it was.

"He's fast asleep, or drunk, or dead; I don't know which," he called to the other oarsman, as he got hold of the steering gear and headed the boat upstream again. His companion made no reply, and the party proceeded in silence to the landing. Here, by dint of much shouting and hallooing, the inmates of a house close by became informed of something unusual outside, and, after a suitable delay, a man appeared, carrying a lantern.

"It's you, is it?" he said to the mail carrier. "I reckoned you wouldn't cross tonight. Who ye got in there?"

"It's Joe Chillis. We picked him up outside, about a mile off the land. His boat had been upset, en' he'd lost an oar, en' ef we hadn't gone to his assistance, it would have been the last of old Joe, I guess."

"Hullo, Joe! Why don't you git up?" asked the man, seeing that Chillis did not rise or change his position.

"By George! I don't know what's the matter with him. Give me the lantern," and the mail carrier took the light and flashed it over Chillis's face.

"I don't know whether he's asleep, or has fainted, or what. He's awful white, an' there's an ugly cut in his shoulder, en' his coat's all torn away. Must have hurt himself tryin' to right his boat, I guess. George! The iron on the rowlock must have struck right into the flesh."

"He didn't say he was hurt," rejoined the other oarsman.

"It's like enough he didn't know it," said the man with the lantern. "When a man's in danger he doesn't feel a hurt. Poor old Joe! He wasn't drunk, or he couldn't have handled his boat at all in this weather. We must take him in, I s'pose."

Then the three men lifted him upon his feet and, by shaking and talking, aroused him sufficiently to walk with their support to the house. There they laid him on a bench and brought him a glass of hot whiskey and water, and the women of the house gathered about shyly, gazing compassionately upon the ugly wound in the odd man's delicate white flesh, white and delicate as the fairest woman's.

Presently, Chillis sat up and looked about him. "Have you got me the oars?" he said to the mail carrier.

"You won't row any more tonight, Joe, *I* guess," the carrier answered, smiling grimly. "Look at your shoulder, man."

"Shoulder be d—d!" retorted Chillis. "Beg pardon, ladies; I didn't see you. Been asleep, haven't I? Perhaps, sence you seem to think I'm not fit for rowin', one of these ladies will do me the favor to help me put myself in order. Have you a piece of court plaster or a healing salve, ma'am?" he said to the elder woman. "Ladies mostly keep sech trifles about them, I believe."

Then he straightened himself up to his magnificent height and threw out his broad, round chest, as if the gash in his shoulder were an epaulet or a band of stars instead.

"Of course, I can do something for you," said the woman he had addressed, very cheerfully and quickly. "I have the best healing salve in all the country." Running away, she quickly returned with a roll of linen and the invaluable salve.

"I must look at the wound and see if it wants washing out. Ugh! O, dear! It is a dreadful cut and ragged. You will have to go to the doctor with that, I'm afraid. But I'll just put this on tonight to prevent your taking cold in it, though you will take cold, anyway, if you do not get a change of clothes." The good woman looked round at her husband, asking him with her eyes to offer this very necessary kindness.

"You'll stop with us tonight, Joe," said the man, in answer to this appeal, "an' the sooner you git off them wet clothes the better. I'll lend you some o' mine."

"Yes, indeed, Mr. Chillis, you must get out of these wet things and put on some of Ben's. Then you will let me get you a bit of hot supper and go right to bed. You don't look as if you could sit up. There!" she added, as the salve was pressed gently down over the torn flesh, and heaving a deep sigh, "if you feel half as sick as I do, just looking at it, you will do well to get ready to lie down."

"Thankee, ma'am. It's worth a man's while to git hurt a leetle, ef he has a lady to take care o' him," answered Chillis, gallantly. "But I can't accept your kindness any furder tonight. Ef I can git the loan of a lantern an' a pair o' oars, it is all I ask, for home I must go, as soon as possible."

"Ben will lend you a lantern," said the mail carrier, "an' I will lend you the oars, as I promised, but what on earth you want to go any further in this storm for, beats me."

"This storm has only jist begun, and it's goin' to last three days," returned Chillis. "No use waitin' for it to quit, so, good-night to you all. I've made a pretty mess o' your floor," he added, turning to glance at the little black puddles that had drained out of his great spongy blanket coat and run down through his leaky boots onto the white-scoured boards of the kitchen; then, glancing from them to the mistress of the house he said, "I hope you'll excuse me." And with that he opened the door quickly and shut himself out into the tempest once more, making his way by the lantern's aid to the boathouse at the landing, where he helped himself to what he needed and was soon pulling up the creek. Luckily there was no current against him, for it was sickening work making the oar-stroke with that hurt in his shoulder.

He could see by the light of the lantern, which he occasionally held aloft, that the long grass of the tidemarsh was already completely submerged, the immense flats looking like a sea, with the wind driving the water before it in long rolls or catching it up and flirting it through the air in spray and foam. His only guide to his course was the scattering line of low willows whose tops still bent and shook above the flood, indicating the slightly raised banks of the creek, everything more distant being hidden in the profound darkness which brooded over and seemed a part of the storm. But even with these landmarks he wandered a good deal in his reckoning, and an hour or more had elapsed before his watchful eyes caught the gleam of what might have been a star reflected in the ocean.

"Thank God!" he whispered and pulled a little faster toward that spark of light.

In ten minutes more, he moored his boat to the hitching-post in front of a tiny cottage, from whose uncurtained window the light of a brisk wood fire was shining. As the chain clanked in the ring, the door opened, and a woman and child looked out.

"Is that you, Eben?" asked the woman, in an eager voice, made husky by previous weeping. "I certainly feared you were drowned." Then seeing, as her eyes became accustomed to the darkness, that the figure still lingering about the boat was not her husband's, she shrank back, fearing the worst.

"I'm sorry I'm not the one you looked for, Mrs. Smiley," answered Chillis, standing on the bit of portico, with its dripping honeysuckle vines swinging in the wind, "but I'm better than nobody, I reckon, an' Smiley will hardly be home tonight. The bay's awful rough, an' ef I hadn't started over early, I shouldn't have ventured, neither. No, you needn't look for your husband tonight, ma'am."

"Will you not come in by the fire, Mr. Chillis?" asked the woman, hesitatingly, seeing that he seemed waiting to be invited.

"Thankee. But I shall spile your floor ef I do. I'm a perfect sponge, not fit to come near a lady, nohow. I thought," he added, as he closed the door and advanced to the hearth, "that I would jest stop an' see ef I could do anything for you, seein' as I guessed you'd be alone, and mebbe afeard o' the storm an' the high tide. Ladies mostly is afeard to be alone at sech times," he said, untying the yellow cotton handkerchief and throwing his sodden hat upon the stone hearth.

"Do you think there is any danger?" asked Mrs. Smiley, embarrassed, yet anxious. She stood in the middle of the room, behind him, with that irresolute air an inexperienced person has in unexpected circumstances.

He turned around with his back to the blaze, while a faint mist of evaporation began to creep out all over him and occasionally to dart out in slender streams and float up the wide chimney.

"There's no danger *now*, an' mebbe there won't *be* any. But the tide will not turn much afore midnight, an' it's higher now than it generally is when it is full."

"What's that?" cried Willie, the boy, his senses sharpened by the mention of danger.

"It's the wind rattlin' my boat chains," returned Chillis, smiling at the little fellow's startled looks.

"Your boat chain!" echoed his mother, not less startled. "Was it your boat that you were fastening to the hitching-post? I thought it was your horse. Is the water up so high, then, already?" she said, her cheeks paling as she spoke.

"I dragged it up a little way," returned Chillis, slowly, and turning his face back to the fire. He was listening attentively and thought he caught the sound of lapping water.

"Have you just come from Astoria?" asked Mrs. Smiley, approaching, and standing at one corner of the hearth. The firelight shone full upon her now and revealed a clear white face; large, dark-gray eyes, full of sadness and perplexity; a beautifully shaped head, coiled round and round with heavy twists of golden hair that glittered in its highlights like burnished metal; and a figure at once full and lithe in its proportions, clad in a neat-fitting dress of some soft dark material, set off with a tiny white collar and bright ribbon. It was easy to see why she was the "White Rose" to the rough old mountain man. She was looking up at him with an eager, questioning gaze that meant, O, ever so much more than her words.

"Not quite direct. I stopped down at the landin', an' I lost a little time gittin' capsized in the bay. I left about three o'clock."

"Might not Eben have left a little later," the gray eyes added, "and have been capsized, too?"

"He wouldn't *try* to cross half an hour later—I'll wager my head on that. He can't get away from town tonight, an', what is worse, I don't think he can cross for two or three days. We've got our Christmas storm on hand, an' a worse one than we've had for twenty years, or I'm mistaken."

"If you thought the storm was going to be severe, why did you not warn Eben, Mr. Chillis?" The gray eyes watched him steadily.

"I did say there would be a sou'-wester uncommon severe, but Rumway laughed at me for prophesyin' in his company. Besides, I was in a hurry to get off, myself, and wouldn't argue with 'em. Smiley's a man to take his own way pretty much, too."

"I wish you had warned him," sighed Mrs. Smiley, and turned wearily away. She left her guest gazing into the fire and, still steaming in a very unsavory manner, lighted a candle, set it in the window, and opened the door to look out. What she saw made her start back with a cry of affright and hurriedly close the door.

"Your boat is this side of the hitching-post, and the water is all around us!"

"An' it is not yet eight o'clock. I guessed it would be so."

Just then, a fearful blast shook the house, and the boat's chain clanked nearer. Willie caught his mother's hand and shivered all over with terror. "O, mamma!" he sobbed, "will the water drown our house?"

"I hope not, my boy. It may come up and wet our warm, dry floor, but I trust it will not give us so much trouble. We do not like wet feet, do we, Willie?"

Then the mother, intent on soothing the child, sat down in the firelight and held his curly head in her lap, whispering little cooing sentences into his ear whenever he grew restless, while her strange, unbidden guest continued to evaporate in one corner of the hearth, sitting with his hands on his knees, staring at something in the coals. There was no attempt at conversation. There had never, until this evening, been a dozen words exchanged between these neighbors, who knew each other by sight and by reputation well enough. Joe Chillis was not a man whose personal appearance, so far as clothes went, nor whose reputation, would commend him to women generally—the one being shabby and careless, the other smacking of recklessness and whiskey. Not that any great harm was known of the man, but that he was out of the pale of polite society even in this new and isolated corner of the earth. He had had an Indian wife in his youth, being more accustomed to the ways of her people than of his own. For nearly twenty years he had lived a thriftless, bachelor existence, known among men, and by hearsay among women, as a noted storyteller and genial, devil-may-care, old mountain man, whose heart was in the right place, but who never drew very heavily upon his brain resources, except to embellish a tale of his early exploits in Indian-fighting, bear-killing, and beaver-trapping. It was with a curious feeling of wonder that Mrs. Smiley found herself *téte-a-téte* with him at her own fireside, and, in spite of her anxiety about other matters, she could not help studying him a good deal as he sat there, silent and almost as motionless as a statue; nor keep from noticing his splendid *physique* and the aristocratic cut of his features; nor from imagining him as he must have been in his youth. She was absorbed for a little while, picturing this gallant young White among his Indian associates—trying to fancy how he treated his squaw wife, and whether he really cared for her as he would for a White woman; then, she wondered what kind of an experience his present life would be for anyone else—herself, for instance—living most of the year on a flatboat housed in, and hiding in sloughs, and all manner of watery, out-of-the-way places. She loved forest and stream, and sylvan shades, well enough, but not well enough for that. So a human creature who could thus voluntarily exile himself must be peculiar. But Joe Chillis did not look peculiar; he looked as alive and human as anybody—in fact, particularly alive and human just now, and it was not any eccentricity which had brought him to her this night, but a real human reason. What was the reason?

What with his mother's cooing whispers and the passing of her light hand over his hair, Willie had fallen asleep. Mrs. Smiley lifted him in her arms and laid him on the lounge, covering him carefully and touching him tenderly, kissing his bright curls at the last. Chillis turned to watch her—he could not help it. Perhaps he speculated about *her* way of living and acting, as she had speculated about his. Meantime, the tempest outside increased in fury, and the little cottage trembled with its fitful shocks.

Now that Willie was asleep, Mrs. Chillis felt a growing nervousness and embarrassment. She could not bring herself to sit down again, alone with Joe Chillis. Not that she was afraid of him— there was nothing in his appearance to inspire a dread of the man, but she wanted to know what he was there for. The sensitive nerves of the man felt this mental inquiry of hers, but he would not be the first to speak, so he let her flutter about—brightening the fire, putting to right things that were right enough as they were, and making a pretense of being busied with household cares. At length, there was nothing more to do except to wind the clock, which stood on the mantel over the hearth. Here was her opportunity.

"The evening has seemed very long," she said, "but it is nine o'clock, at last."

Chillis got up, went to the door, and opened it. The boat was bumping against the floor of the tiny portico. She saw it, too, and her heart gave a great bound. Chillis came back and sat down by the fire, looking very grave and preoccupied. With a little shiver, she sat down opposite. It was clear that he had no intention of going, and, strange as she felt the situation to be, she experienced a sort of relief that he was there. She was not a cowardly woman, nor was her guest one she would have been likely to appeal to in any peril, but, since a possible peril had come, and he was there of his own accord, she owned to herself she was not sorry. She was a woman, anyway, and must need the required services of men, whoever they might be. Having disposed of this question, it occurred to her to be gracious to the man whose services she had made up her mind to accept. Glancing into his face, she noticed its pallor, and then remembered what he had said about being capsized in the bay, and that he was an old man, and then, that he might not have had any supper. All of which inspired her to say, "I beg pardon, Mr. Chillis. I presume you have eaten nothing this evening. I shall get you something, right away—a cup of hot coffee, for instance." And, without waiting to hear his faint denial, Mrs. Smiley made all haste to put her hospitable intentions into practice, and soon had spread a little table with a very appetizing array of cold meats, fruit, bread, and coffee.

While her guest, with a few words of thanks, accepted and disposed of the refreshments, Mrs. Smiley sat and gazed at the fire in her turn. The little cottage trembled, the windows rattled, the storm roared without, and—yes, the water actually lapped against the house! She started, turning to the door. The wind was driving the flood in under it. She felt a chill run through her flesh.

"Mr. Chillis, the water is really coming into the house!"

"Yes, I reckoned that it would," returned the old man, calmly, rising from the table and returning to the hearth. "That is the nicest supper I've had for these dozen years, and it has done me good, too. I was a little wore out with pullin' over the bay, aginst the wind."

Mrs. Smiley looked at him curiously and then at the water splashing in under the door. He understood her perfectly.

"A wettin' wouldn't hurt you, though it would be disagreeable, an' I should be sorry to have you put to that inconvenience. But the wind *and* the water may unsettle the foundation o' your house, the chimney bein' on the outside, an' no support to it. Even that would not certainly put you in danger, as the frame would likely float. But I knew ef sech a thing should happen, an' you here alone, you would be very much frightened, an' perhaps lose your life a-tryin' to save it."

"And you came up from the landing in all this storm to take care of me?" Mrs. Smiley exclaimed, with flushing cheeks.

"I came all the way from Astoria to do it," answered Chillis, looking at the new-blown roses of her face.

"And Eben—" She checked herself and fixed her eyes upon the hearth.

"He thought there was no danger, most likely."

"Mr. Chillis, I can never thank you!" she cried fervently, as she turned to glance at the sleeping child.

"White Rose," he answered, under his breath, "I don't want any thanks but those I've got." Then, aloud to her, "You might have some blankets ready, in case we are turned out o' the house. The fire will be 'most sure to be put out, anyway, an' you an' the boy will be cold."

Mrs. Smiley was shivering with that tenseness of the nerves that the bravest women suffer from when obliged to wait the slow but certain approach of danger. Her teeth chattered together as she went about her bandbox of a house, collecting things that would be needed, should she be forced to abandon the shelter of its lowly roof, and, as she was thus engaged, she thought the place had never seemed so cosy as it did this wild and terrible night. She put on her rubber overshoes, tied snugly on a pretty woollen hood, got ready a pile of blankets and a warm shawl, lighted a large glass lantern (as she saw the water approaching the fireplace), and, last, proceeded to arouse Willie and wrap him up in overcoat, little fur cap, and warm mittens; when all was done, she turned and looked anxiously at the face of her guest. It might have been a mask, for all she could learn from it. He was silently watching her, not looking either depressed or hopeful. She went up to him and touched his sleeve. "How wet you are, still," she said, compassionately. "I had forgotten that you must have been uncomfortable after your capsize in the bay. Perhaps it is not too late to change your clothes. You will find some of Eben's in the next room. Shall I lay them out for you?"

He smiled when she touched him, a bright, warm smile that took away ten years of his age, but he did not move.

"No," said he, "it's no use now to put on dry clothes. It won't hurt me to be wet; I'm used to it, but I shall be sorry when this cheerful fire is out."

He had hardly spoken when a blast struck the house, more terrific than any that had gone before it, and a narrow crack became visible between the hearthstone and the door, through which the water oozed in quite rapidly. Mrs. Smiley's face blanched.

"That started the house a leetle," said Chillis, lighting his lantern by the fire.

"Could we get to the landing, do you think?" asked Mrs. Smiley, springing instinctively to the lounge, where the child lay in a half-slumber.

"Not afore the tide begins to run out. Ef it was daylight, we might, by keepin' out o' the channel, but the best we can do now is to stick to the place we're in as long as it holds together or keeps right side up. When we can't stay no longer, we'll take to the boat."

139

"I believe you know best, Mr. Chillis, but it's frightful waiting for one's house to float away from under one's feet or fall about one's head. And the tide, too! I have always feared and bated the tides; they have been a horror to me ever since I came here. It seems so dreadful to have the earth slowly sinking into the sea, for that is the way it appears to do, you know."

"Yes, I remember hearin' you say you were nervous about the tides, once, when I called here to see your husband. Curious, that I often thought o' that chance sayin' o' yours, isn't it?"

Mrs. Smiley's reply was a smothered cry of terror as another blast—sudden, strong, protracted—pushed the house still further away from the fireplace, letting the storm in at the opening, for it was from that direction that the wind came.

"Now she floats!" exclaimed Chillis. "We'll soon know whether she's seaworthy or not. I had better take a look at my boat, I reckon, for that's our last resort, in case your ark is worthless, Mrs. Smiley." He laughed softly and stepped more vigorously than he had done, as the danger grew more certain.

"All right yet—cable not parted; ready to do us a good turn, if we need it."

"We shall not be floated off to the bay, shall we?" asked Mrs. Smiley, trying to smile too.

"Not afore the tide turns, certain."

"It seems to me that I should feel safer anywhere than here. Unseen dangers always are harder to battle with, even in imagination. I do not wish to put you to any further trouble, but I should not mind the storm and the open boat so much as seeing my house going to pieces with me in it—and Willie."

"I've been a-thinkin'," replied Chillis, "that the house, after all, ain't goin' to be much protection, with the water splashin' under foot, an' the wind an' rain drivin' in on that side where the chimney is took away. It's an awful pity such a neat, nice little place should come to grief, like this—a real snug little home!"

"And what else were you thinking?" she asked, bringing him back to the subject of expedients.

"You mentioned goin' to the landin'. Well, we can't go there, for I doubt ef I could find the way in the dark, with the water over the tops of the bushes on the creek bank. Besides, in broad daylight it would be tough work, pullin' agin' the flood, an' I had the misfortin to hurt my shoulder tryin' to right my boat in the bay, which partly disables me, I am sorry to say, for I should like to put my whole strength to your service."

"O, Mr. Chillis! Say no more, I beg. How selfish I am! When you have been so kind—with a bruise on your shoulder and all! Cannot I do anything for you? I have liquor in the closet, if you would like to bathe with it."

"See—she moves again!" cried he, as the house swayed yet further away from the smouldering fire. "I've heard of abandonin' one's hearthstone, but I'd no idea that was the way they done it."

"I had best get the brandy, anyway, I think. We may need it if we are forced to go into the boat. But do let me do something for you now, Mr. Chillis? It seems cruel that you have been in your wet clothes for hours, and tired and bruised besides."

"Thankee—'tain't no use!" he said, as she offered him the brandy flask. "The lady down at the landin' put on a plaster, as you can see for yourself," he continued, throwing back the corner of a cloth cape the woman had placed over his shoulders to cover the rent in his coat. "The doctor will have to fix it up, I reckon, for it is cut up pretty bad with the iron."

Mrs. Smiley turned suddenly sick. She was just at that stage of excitement when "a rose-leaf on the beaker's brim" causes the overflow of the cup. The undulations of the water, under the floor and over it, contributed still further to the feeling, and she hurried to the lounge to save herself from falling. Here she threw herself beside Willie and cried a little, quietly, under cover of her shawl.

"There she goes! Well, this isn't pleasant, noways," said Chillis, as the house, freed with a final crash from impediments, swayed about unsteadily, impelled by wind and water. "I was sayin' a bit ago that we could not git to the landin' at present. There are three ways o' choosin', though, which are these: to stay where we are; to git into the boat, en' let the house take its chances; or to try to git to my cabin, where we would be safe an' could keep warm."

"How long would it take us to get to your house?" asked Mrs. Smiley, from under her shawl.

"An hour, mebbe. We should have to feel our way."

Mrs. Smiley reflected. Sitting out in an open boat, without trying to do anything, would be horrible; staying where she was would be hardly less so. It would be six or seven hours still to daylight. There was no chance of the storm abating, though the water must recede after midnight.

"Let us go," she said, sitting up. "You will not desert *me*, I know, and why should I keep you here all night in anxiety and peril? Once at home, you can rest and nurse yourself."

"So be it; an' God help us!"

"Amen!"

Chillis opened the door and looked out, placing a light first in the window. Then coming back for a basin, he waded out, bailed his boat, and, unfastening the chain, hauled it alongside the doorway. Mrs. Smiley had hastily put some provisions into a tin bucket, with a cover, and some things for Willie into another, and stood holding them, ready to be stowed away.

"You will have to take the tiller," said Chillis, placing the buckets safely in the boat.

"I meant to take an oar," said she.

"If you know how to steer, it will be better for me to pull alone. Now, let us have the boy, right in the bottom here, with plenty o' blankets under and over him; the same for yourself. The lanterns—so. Now, jump in!"

"The fire is dead on the hearth," she said, looking back through the empty house and across the gap of water showing through the broken wall. "What a horrible scene! God sent you, Mr. Chillis, to help me live through it."

"I believe he did. Are you quite ready?"

"Quite; only tell me what I must do. I wish I could help you."

"You do?" he answered, and then he bent himself to the work before him, with a sense of its responsibility, which exalted it into a deed of the purest chivalry.

PART II

The widow Smiley did not live on Clatsop Plains. Ever since the great storm at Christmas, when her house was carried off its foundations by the high tide, she had refused to go back to it. When the neighbors heard of her husband's death, they took her over to Astoria to see him buried, for there was no home to bring him to, and she had never returned. Smiley, they say, was drowned where he fell, in the streets of Astoria, that night of the high tide, being too intoxicated to get up. But nobody told the widow that. They said to her that he stumbled off the wharf, in the dark, and that the tide brought him ashore, and that was enough for her to know.

She was staying with the family at the landing when the news came, two days after his death. Joe Chillis brought her things down to the landing and had them sent over to Astoria, where she decided to stay, and afterward she sold the farm and bought a small house in town, where, after two or three months, she opened a school for young children. And the women of the place had all taken to making much of Joe Chillis, in consideration of his conduct during that memorable time and of his sufferings in consequence, for he was laid up a long while afterward with that hurt in his shoulder and the consequences of his exposure. Mrs. Smiley always treated him with the highest respect, and did not conceal that she had a great regard for him, if he *was* nothing but an old mountain man who had had a squaw wife, which regard, under the circumstances, was not to be wondered at.

Widow Smiley was young, and pretty, and *smart,* and Captain Rumway, the pilot, was dreadfully taken up with her, and nobody would blame her for taking a second husband who was able and willing to provide well for her. If it was to be a match, nobody would speak a word against it. It was said that he had left off drinking on her account and was building a fine house up on the hill, on one of the prettiest lots in town. Such was the gossip about Mrs. Smiley, a year and a half after the night of the high tide.

It was the afternoon of a July day in Astoria, and, since we have given the reader so dismal a picture of December, let us, in justice, say a word about this July day. All day long the air had been as bright and clear as crystal, and the sun had sparkled on the blue waters of the noblest of rivers without blinding the eyes with glare, or sickening the senses with heat. Along either shore rose lofty highlands, crowned with cool-looking forests of dark-green firs. Far to the east, like a cloud on the horizon, the snowy cone of St. Helen's mountain stood up above the wooded heights of the Cascade Range, with Mount Adams peeping over its shoulder. Quite near, and partly closing off the view up the river, was picturesque Tongue Point—a lovely island of green—connected with the shore only by a low and narrow isthmus. From this promontory to the point below the town, the bank of the river was curtained and garlanded with blossoming shrubs—mock-orange, honeysuckle, spirea, aerifolia, crimson roses, and clusters of elderberries, lavender, scarlet, and orange—everywhere, except where men had torn them away to make room for their improvements.

Looking seaward, there was the long line of white surf that marks where sea and river meet, miles away, with the cape and lighthouse tower standing out in sharp relief against the expanse of ocean beyond, and sailing vessels lying off the bar waiting for Rumway and his associates to come off and show them the entrance between the sand-spits. And nearer, all about on the surface of the sparkling river, snowy sails were glancing in the sun like the wings of birds that skim beside them. It is hard, in July, to believe it has ever been December.

Perhaps Mrs. Smiley was thinking so, from her rose-embowered cottage porch on the hill, not far from Captain Rumway's new house, as she watched the sun sinking in a golden glory behind the lighthouse and the cape. Her school dismissed for the week and her household tasks completed, she was taking her repose in a great sleepy-hollow of a chair, near enough to the roses to catch their delicate fragrance. Her white dress looked fresh and dainty, with a rose-colored ribbon at the throat and a bunch of spirea— sea foam, Willie called it—in her gleaming, braided hair. Her great gray eyes, neither sad nor bright, but sweetly serious, harmonized the delicate pure tones that made up her person and her dress, leaving nothing to be desired, except, perhaps, a suggestion of color in the clear, white oval of her cheeks. And that an accident supplied.

For while the sun yet sent lances of gold up out of the sea, the garden gate clicked, and Captain Rumway came up the wall. He was a handsome man of fine figure, with a bronzed complexion, dark eyes, and hair always becomingly tossed up, owing to a slight wave in it and a springy quality it had of its own. The sun and sea air, while they had bronzed his face, had imparted to his cheeks that rich glow that is often the only thing lacking to make a dark face beautiful. Looking at him, one could hardly help catching something of his glow, if only through admiration of it. Mrs. Smiley's sudden color was possibly to be accounted for on this ground.

"Good evening, Mrs. Smiley," he said, lifting his hat gracefully. "I have come to ask you to walk over and look at my house. No, thank you; I will not come in, if you are ready for the walk. I will stop here and smell these roses while you get your hat."

"Is your house so nearly completed, then?" she asked as they went down the walk together.

"So nearly that I require a woman's opinion upon the inside arrangements; and there is no one whose judgment upon such matters I value more than yours."

"I suppose you mean to imply that I am a good housekeeper? But there is great diversity of taste among good housekeepers, Mr. Rumway."

"Your taste will suit me—that I am sure of. I did not see Willie at home; is he gone away?" he asked, to cover a sudden embarrassing consciousness.

"I let him go home with Mr. Chillis last evening, but I expect him home tonight."

"Poor old Joe! He takes a great deal of comfort with the boy. And no wonder—he is a charming child, worthy of such parentage," he said, glancing at his companion's face.

"I am glad when anything of mine gives Mr. Chillis pleasure," returned Mrs. Smiley, looking straight ahead. "I teach Willie to have a great respect and love for him. It is the least we can do."

Rumway noticed the inclusive *we* and winced. "He is a strange man," he said, by way of answer.

"A hero!" cried Mrs. Smiley firmly.

"And never more so than when in whiskey," added Rumway, ungenerously.

"Younger and more fortunate men have had that fault," she returned, thinking of Eben.

"And conquered it," he added, thinking of himself.

"Here we are. Just step in this doorway a bit and look at the view. Glorious, isn't it? I have sent for a lot of very choice shrubs and trees for the grounds, and mean to make this the prettiest place in town."

"It must be very pretty with this view," replied Mrs. Smiley, drinking in the beauty of the scene with genuine delight.

"Please step inside. Now, it is about the arrangement of the doors, windows, closets, and all that, I wanted advice. I am told that ladies claim to understand these things better than men."

"They ought, I am sure, since the house is alone their realm. What a charming room! So light, so airy, with such a view, and the doors and windows in the right places, too. And this cunning little porch towards the west! I'm glad you have that porch, Mr. Rumway. I have always said every house should have a sunset porch. I enjoy mine so much these lovely summer evenings."

And so they went through the house; she delighted with it, in the main, but making little suggestions, here and there, he palpitating with her praises, as if they had been bestowed on himself. And, indeed, was not this house a part of himself, having so many of his sweetest hopes built into it? For what higher proof does a man give of a worthy love than in constructing a bright and cheerful shelter for the object of it—than in making sure of a fitting home?

"It will lack nothing," she said, as they stood together again on the "sunset porch," talking of grouping the shrubbery as not to intercept the view.

"Except a mistress," he added, turning his eyes upon her face, full of intense meaning. "With the right woman in it, it will seem perfect to me; without her, it is nothing but a monument of my folly. There is but one woman I ever want to see in it. Can you guess who it is? Will you come?"

Mrs. Smiley looked up into the glowing face bent over her, searching the passionate dark eyes with her clear, cool gaze, while slowly the delicate color crept over face and neck, as her eyes fell before his ardent looks, and she drew in her breath quickly.

"I, I do not know; there are so many things to think of."

"What things? Let me help you consider them. If you mean—"

"O, mamma, mamma!" shouted Willie, from the street. "Here we are, and I've had such a splendid time. We've got some fish for you, too. Are you coming right home?" And there, on the sidewalk, was Chillis, carrying a basket with his hat stuck full of flowers, and as regardless as a child of the drollery of his appearance.

Mrs. Smiley started a little as she caught the expression of his face, thinking it did not comport with the holiday appearance of his habiliments, and hastened at once to obey its silent appeal. Rumway walked beside her to the gate.

"Have you no answer for me?" he asked hurriedly.

"Give me a week," she returned, and slipped away from him, taking the basket from Chillis and ordering Willie to carry it, while she walked by the old man's side.

"You have been lookin' at your new house?" he remarked. "You need not try to hide your secret from me. I see it in your face—" and he looked long and wistfully upon the rosy record.

"If you see something in *my* face, I see something in yours. You have a trouble, a new pain of some kind. Yesterday you looked forty and radiant; this evening your face is white and drawn by suffering."

"You do observe the old man's face sometimes, then? That other has not quite blotted it out? O, my lovely lady! How sweet an' dainty you look in that white dress. It does my old eyes good to look at you."

"You are never too ill or sad to make me pretty compliments, Mr. Chillis. Do you know, I think I have grown quite vain since I have had you to flatter me. We constitute a mutual admiration society, I'm sure."

Then she led him into the rose-covered porch and seated him in the "sleepy-hollow," brought him a dish of strawberries, and told him to rest while she got ready his supper.

"Rest!" he answered, "*I'm* not tired. Willie an' I cooked our own supper, too. So you jest put Willie to bed—he's tired enough,

I guess—an' then come an' talk to me. That's all I want tonight—is jest to hear the White Rose talk."

While Mrs. Smiley was occupied with Willie—his wants and his prattle—her guest sat motionless, his head on his hand, his elbow resting on the arm of the chair. He had that rare repose of bearing which is understood to be a sign of high breeding, but in him was temperament, or a quietude caught from nature and solitude. It gave a positive charm to his manner, whether animated or depressed; a dignified, introspective, self-possessed carriage that suited his powerfully built, symmetrical frame and regular cast of features. Yet, self-contained as his usual expression was, his face was capable of vivid illuminations and striking changes of aspect, under the influence of feelings either pleasant or painful. In the shadow of the rose-vines and the gathering twilight, it would have been impossible to discern, by any change of feature, what his meditations might be now.

"The moon is full tonight," said Mrs. Smiley, bringing out her low rocker and placing it near her friend. "It will be glorious on the river, and all the "young folks" will be out, I suppose."

"Did not Rumway ask you to go? Don't let me keep you at home, ef he did."

"No; I am not counted among young folks any longer," returned she, with a little sigh, that might mean something or nothing. Then a silence fell between them for several minutes. It was the fashion of these friends to wait for the spirit to move them to converse, and not unfrequently a silence longer than that which was in heaven came between their sentences, but tonight there was thunder in their spiritual atmosphere, and the stillness was oppressive. Mrs. Smiley beat a tattoo with her slipper.

"Rumway asked you to marry him, did he?" began Chillis, at last, in a low and measured tone.

"Yes."

"An' you accepted him?"

"Not yet," she said in a quavering adagio.

"But you will?"

"Perhaps so. I do not know," she said in a firmer voice.

"Rumway is doin' well, an' he is a pretty good fellow, as men go. But he is not half the man that I was at his age—or, rather, that I might have been, ef I had had sech a motive for bein' a man as he has."

"It is not difficult to believe that, Mr. Chillis. There is heroic material in you, and, I fear, none in Mr. Rumway." She spoke naturally and cheerfully now, as if she had no sentiment too sacred to be revealed about the person in question. "But why was there no motive?"

"Why? It was my fate; there was none—that's all. I had gone off to the mountains when a lad, an' couldn't git back—couldn't even git letters from home. The fur companies didn't allow correspondence—it made their men homesick. When I came to be a man, I did as the other men did, took an Indian wife, an' became the father o' half-breed children. I never expected to live any other way than jest as we lived then—roamin' about the mountains, exposed to dangers continually, an' reckless because it was no use to think. But, after I had been a savage for a dozen years—long enough to ruin any man—the fur companies began to break up. The beaver were all hunted out o' the mountains. The men were ashamed to go home—Indians as we all were—an' so drifted off down here, where it was possible to git somethin' to eat, an' where there was quite a settlement o' retired trappers, missionaries, deserted sailors, and such-like Whites."

"You brought your families with you?"

"Of course. We could not leave them in the mountains, with the children, to starve. Besides, we loved our children. They were not to blame for bein' half-Indian, en' we could not separate them from their mothers ef we had a-wished. We did the only thing we could do under the circumstances—married the mothers by White

150

men's laws—to make the children legitimate. Even the heads of the Hudson's Bay Company were forced to comply with the sentiment of the White settlers, an' their descendants are among the first families of Oregon. But they had money an' position; the trappers had neither, though there were some splendid men among them—so our families were looked down upon. O, White Rose! Didn't I used to have some bitter thoughts in those days? For my blood was high blood in the state where I was raised."

"I can imagine it very easily," said Mrs. Smiley, softly.

"But I never let on. I was wild and devil-may-care. To hide my mortification, I faced it out as well as I could, but I wasn't made, in the beginnin', for that kind o' life, en' it took away my manhood. After the country began to settle up, en' families—real White families—began to move in, I used to be nearly crazy sometimes. Many's the day that I've rode through the woods or over the prairies, tryin' to git away from myself, but I never said a cross word to the squaw wife. Why should I? It was not her fault. Sometimes she fretted at me (the Indian women are great scolds), but I did not answer her back. I displeased her with my vagabond ways, very likely—her White husband, to whom she looked for better things. I couldn't work; I didn't take no interest in work, like other men."

"O, Mr. Chillis! Was not that a great mistake? Would not some kind of ambition have helped to fill up the blank in your life?"

"I didn't have any—I couldn't have any, with that old Indian woman sittin' there, in the corner o' my hearth. When the crazy fit came on, I jest turned my back on home an' mounted my horse for a long, lonely ride, or went to town and drank whiskey till I was past rememberin' my trouble. But I never complained. The men I associated with expected me to amuse them, an' I generally did, with all manner o' wild freaks en' incredible stories—some o' which were truer than they believed, for I had had plenty of adventures in the mountains. White Rose, do you imagine I ever loved that squaw wife o' mine?"

"I remember asking myself such a question, that night of the storm, as you stood by the fire, so still and strange. I was speculating about your history and starting these very queries you have answered tonight."

"But you have never asked me."

"No; how could I? But I am glad to know. Now I understand the great patience—the tender, pathetic patience—that I have often remarked in you. Only those who have suffered long and silently can ever attain to it."

"An' so people say, 'Poor old Joe!' an' they don't know what they mean when they say it. They think I am a man without the ambitions an' passions of other men; a simple, good fellow without too much brain en' only the heart of a fool. But they don't know me—they don't know me!"

"How could they, without hearing what you have just told me or without knowing you as I know you?"

"They never will know. I don't want to be pitied for my mistakes. 'Poor old Joe' is proud as well as poor."

Mrs. Smiley sat silent, gazing at the river's silver ripples. Her shapely hands were folded in her lap, her whole attitude quiet, absorbed. Whether she was thinking of what she had heard or whether she had forgotten it, no one could have guessed from her manner, and Chillis could not wait to know. The fountains of the deep had been stirred until they would not rest.

"Was there no other question you asked yourself about the old mountain man that he can answer? Did you never wonder whether he ever had loved at all?"

"You have made me wonder, tonight, whether, at some period of your life, you have not loved some woman of your own race and color. You must have had some opportunities of knowing White women."

"Very few. An' my pride was agin seekin' what I knew was not for me, for the woman I fancied to myself was no common White woman. White Rose, I carried a young man's heart in my bosom until I was near sixty, *an' then I lost it.*" He put out a hand and touched one of hers, ever so lightly. "I need not tell you any more."

A silence that made their pulses seem audible followed this confession. A heavy shadow descended upon both hearts, and a sudden dreary sense of an unutterable and unalterable sorrow burdened their spirits.

After a little, "Mr. Chillis! Mr. Chillis!" wailed the woman's pathetic voice, and "O, my lovely lady!" sighed the man's.

"What shall I do? What shall I do? I am so sorry. What shall I do?"

"Tell me to go. I knew it would have to end so. I knew that Rumway would drive me to say what I ought not to say, for he is not worthy o' you—no man that I know of is. Ef I was as young as he an' had his chance, I would make myself worthy o' you or die. But it is too late. Old Joe Chillis may starve his heart, as he has many a time starved his body in the desert. But I did love you so! O, my sweet White Rose, I did love you so! Always, from the first time I saw you."

"What is that you say?" said Mrs. Smiley, in a shocked voice.

"Always, I said, from the first time I saw you. My love was true; it did not harm you. I said, *'There* is such a woman as God designed for me. But it is too late to have her now. I will jest worship her humbly, a great ways off, an' say "God bless her!" when she passes, an' think o' her sweet ways when I am ridin' through the woods or polin' my huntin' boat up the sloughs, among the willow an' pond lilies. She would hardly blame me, ef she knew I loved her that way.'

"But it grew harder afterwards, White Rose, when you were grateful to me, in your pretty, womanly way, an' treated me so kindly before all the world, an' let your little boy love me, an' loved me yourself—I knew it—in a gentle, friendly fashion. O, but it was sweet—but not sweet enough, sometimes. Ef I have been crazed for the lack o' love in my younger days, I have been crazed with love since then. There have been days when I could neither work nor eat, nights when I could not sleep, for thinkin' o' what might have been but never could be; times when I have been tempted to upset my boat in the bay an' never try to right it. But when I had almost conquered my madness, that you might never know, then comes this Rumway, with his fine looks, an' his fine house, an' his fine professions, an' blots me out entirely, for what will old Joe be worth to Madame Rumway, or to Madame Rumway's fine husband?"

Mrs. Smiley sat thoughtful and silent a long time after this declaration of love that gave all and required so little. She was sorry for it, but since it was so, and she must know it, she was glad that she had heard it that night. She could place it in the balance with that other declaration and decide upon their relative value to her, for she saw, as he did, that the two were incompatible—one must be given up.

"It is late," she said, rising. "You will come up and take breakfast with Willie and me before you go home? My strawberries are in their prime."

"I thought you would a-told me to go an' never come back," he said, stepping out into the moonlight with the elastic tread of twenty-five. He stopped and looked back at her with a beaming countenance, like a boy's.

She was standing on the step above him, looking down at him with a pleasant but serious expression. "I am going to trust you never to repeat to me what you have said tonight. I know I can trust you."

"So be it, White Rose," he returned, with so rapid and involuntary a change of attitude, voice, and expression, that the pang of his hurt pierced her heart also. But "I know I can trust you," she repeated, as if she had not seen that shrinking from the blow. "And I am going to try to make your life a little pleasanter and more like other people's. When you are dressed up and ordered to behave properly and made to look as handsome as you can, so that ladies shall take notice of you and flatter you with their eyes and tongues, and you come to have the same interest in the world that other men have—and why shouldn't you?—then your imagination will not be running away with you or making angels out of common little persons like myself—how dreadfully prosy and commonplace you have no idea! And I forbid you to allow Willie to stick your hat full of flowers when you go fishing together and order you to make that young impudence respectful to you on all occasions—asserting your authority, if necessary. And, lastly, I prefer you should not call me Madame Rumway until I have a certified and legal claim to the title. Good-night."

He stood bareheaded, his face drooping and half-concealed, pulling the withered flowers out of his hat. Slowly he raised it, made a military salute, and placed it on his head. "It is for you to command and me to obey," he said.

"Breakfast at seven o'clock precisely," called out the tuneful voice of Mrs. Smiley after him, as he went down the garden path with bent head, walking more like an old man than she had ever seen him. Then she went into the house, closed it carefully, after the manner of lone women, and went up to her room. But deliciously cool and fragrant as was the tiny chamber, Mrs. Smiley could not sleep that night. Nor did Chillis come to breakfast next morning.

A month passed away. Work was suspended on Mr. Rumway's house, the doors and windows boarded up, and the gate locked. Everybody knew it could mean but one thing—that Mrs. Smiley had refused the owner. But the handsome captain put a serene face upon it and kept about his business industriously and like a gentleman. The fact that he did not return to his wild courses was remarked upon as something hardly to be credited, but greatly to his honor, for it was universally conceded that such a disappointment as his was enough to drive almost any man to drink who had indulged in it previously; such is the generally admitted frailty of man's moral constitution.

Toward the last of August, Mrs. Smiley received a visit from Chillis. He was dressed with more than his customary regard to appearances and looked a little paler and thinner than usual. Otherwise, he was just the same as ever, and, with no questions asked or answered on either side, their old relations were re-established, and Willie was rapturously excited with the prospect of more Saturday excursions. Yet there was this difference in their manner toward each other—that he now seldom addressed her as "White Rose," and never as "my lovely lady," while it was she who made graceful little compliments to him, and was always gay and bright in his company, and constantly watchful of his comfort or pleasure. She prevailed upon him, too, to make calls with her upon other ladies and gave him frequent commissions that would bring him in contact with a variety of persons. But she could not help seeing that it was only in obedience to her wishes that he made calls or mingled with the town-people, and when, one evening, returning together from a visit where he had been very much patronized, he had remarked, with a shrug and smile of self-contempt, "It is no use, Mrs. Smiley—oil en' water won't mix," she had given it up and never more interfered with his old habits.

So the summer passed, and winter came again, with its long rains, dark days, and sad associations. Although Mrs. Smiley was not at all a "weakly woman," constant effort and care, and the absence of anything very flattering in her future or inspiring in her present, wore upon her, exhausting her vitality too rapidly for perfect health, as the constantly increasing delicacy of her appearance testified. In truth, when the spring opened, she found herself so languid and depressed as to be hardly able to teach, in addition to her housework. Then it was that the gossips took up her case once more and declared, with considerable unanimity, that Mrs. Smiley was pining for the handsome Captain after all, and, if ever she had refused him, was sorry for it—thus revenging themselves upon a woman audacious enough to refuse a man many others would have thought "good enough for them" and "too good for" so unappreciative a person.

With the first bright and warm weather, Willie went to spend a week with his friend, and Mrs. Smiley felt forced to take a vacation. A yachting party were going over to the cape, and Captain Rumway was to take them out over the bar. Rumway himself sent an invitation to Mrs. Smiley—this being the first offer of amity he had felt able to make since the previous July. She laughed a little to herself when the note came (for she was not ignorant of the town-tattle—what school-teacher ever is?) and sent an acceptance. If Captain Rumway were half as courageous as she, the chatterers would be confounded, she promised herself, as she made her toilet for the occasion—not too nice for sea water, but bright and pretty and becoming, as her toilets always were.

So she sailed over to the cape with the "young folks" and, as widows can—particularly widows who have gossip to avenge— was more charming than any girl of them all to the others beside Captain Rumway. The officers of the garrison vied with each other in showing her attentions, and the lighthouse keeper, in exhibiting the wonders and beauties of the place, always, if unconsciously, appealed to Mrs. Smiley for admiration and appreciation. Yet she wore her honors modestly, contriving to share this homage with some other and never accepting it as all meant for herself. And toward Captain Rumway her manner was as absolutely free from either coquetry or awkwardness as that of the most indifferent acquaintance. Nobody, seeing her perfectly frank yet quiet and cool deportment with her former suitor, could say, without falsehood, that she in any way concerned herself about him, and if he had heard that she was pining for him, he was probably undeceived during that excursion. Thus she came home feeling that she had vindicated herself, and with a pretty color in her face that made her look as girlish as any young lady of them all.

But, if Captain Rumway had reopened an acquaintance with Mrs. Smiley out of compassion for any woes she might be suffering on his account, or out of a design to show how completely he was master of himself, or, in short, for any motive whatever, he was taken in his own devices and compelled to surrender unconditionally. Like the man in Scripture, out of whom the devils were cast only to return, his last estate was worse than the first, as he was soon compelled to acknowledge, and one of the first signs of this relapse into fatuity was the resumption of work on the unfinished house and the ornamentation of the neglected grounds.

"I will make it such a place as she cannot refuse," he said to himself, more or less hopefully. "She will have to accept the house and grounds, with me thrown in. And whatever she is pining for, she *is* pining, *that* I can see. It may be for outdoor air and recreation and the care that only a husband can give her. If it be that she can take them along with me."

Thus it was, that when Chillis brought Willie home from his long visit to the woods and streams, he saw the workmen busy on the Captain's house. He heard, too, about the excursion to the cape and the inevitable comments upon Rumway's proceedings. But he said nothing about it to Mrs. Smiley, though he spent the evening in the snug little parlor, and they talked together of many things personally interesting to both, especially about Willie's education and profession in life.

"He ought to go to college," said his mother. "I wish him to be a scholarly man, whatever profession he decides upon afterward. I could not bear that he should not have a liberal education."

"Yes, Willie must be a gentleman," said Chillis, "for his mother's sake he must be that."

"But how to provide the means to furnish such an education as he ought to have is what puzzles me," continued Mrs. Smiley, pausing in her needlework to study that problem more closely and gazing absently at the face of her guest. "Will ten years more of school-teaching do it, I wonder?"

"Ten years o' school-teachin' an' housework an' sewin'!" cried he. "Yes, long before that you will be under the sod o' the graveyard! *You* cannot send the boy to college."

"Who, then?" she said, smiling at his vehemence.

"*I* will."

"You, Mr. Chillis? I thought..." She checked herself, fearing to hurt his pride.

"You thought I was poor, an' so I am, for I never tried to make money. *I* don't want money. But there is land belongin' to me out in the valley—five or six hundred acres—an' land is growin' more valuable every year. Ten years from now I reckon mine would pay a boy's schoolin'. So you needn't work yourself to death for that, Mrs. Smiley."

The tears sprang to the gray eyes, which were turned upon him with such eloquent looks. "It is like you," she said, in a broken voice, "and I have nothing to say."

"You are welcome to my land, White Rose, an' there is nothin' *to* be said."

Then she bent her head over her sewing, feeling, indeed, that there was little use for words.

"Do you know," he asked, breaking a protracted silence, "that you have got to give up teachin'?"

"And do what? I might take to gardening. That would be better, perhaps; I have thought about it."

"Let me see your hands. They look like gardenin': two rose-leaves! Don't it make me wish to be back in my prime? Work for you! Wouldn't I love to work for you?"

"And do you not, in every way you can? Am I to have no pride about accepting so much service? What a poor creature you must take me for, Mr. Chillis."

"There is nothin' else in the world that I think of, nothin' else that I live for, an' after all it is so little, that I cannot save you from spoilin' your pretty looks with care. An' you have troubled yourself about me, too; don't think I haven't seen it. You fret your lovely soul about the old man's trouble, when you can't help it—you, nor nobody. An', after all, what does it matter about *me*? *I* am nothin', and you are everything. I want you to remember that and do everything for your own happiness without wastin' thought on me. I am content to keep my distance, ef I only see you happy and well off. Do you understand me?"

Mrs. Smiley looked up with a suffused face. "Mr. Chillis," she answered, "you make me ashamed of myself and my selfishness. Let us never refer to this subject again. Work don't hurt me, and since you have offered to provide for Willie's education, you have lifted half my burden. Why should you stand at a distance to see me happier than I am, when I am so happy as to have such a friend as you? How am I to be happier by your being at a distance, who have been the kindest of friends? You are out of spirits this evening, and you talk just a little—nonsense." And she smiled at him in a sweetly apologetic fashion for the word.

"That is like enough," he returned gravely, "but I want you to remember my words, foolish or not. Don't let me stand in your light—not for one minute, and don't forget this: that Joe Chillis is happy when he sees the White Rose bloomin' and bright."

Contrary to his command, Mrs. Smiley did endeavor to forget these words in the weeks following, when the old mountain man came no more to her rose-embowered cottage, and when Captain Rumway invented many ingenious schemes for getting the pale schoolteacher to take more recreation and fresh air. She endeavored to forget them, but she could not, though her resolve to ignore them was as strong as it ever had been when her burdens had seemed lighter! But in spite of her resolve, and in spite of the fact that it could not be said that any encouragement had been given to repeat his addresses, Rumway continued to work at his house and grounds steadily and, to all appearance, hopefully. And although he never consulted Mrs. Smiley now concerning the arrangement of either, he showed that he remembered her suggestions of the year before by following them out without deviation.

Thus quietly, without incident, the June days slipped away, and the perfect July weather returned once more, when there was always a chair or two out on the sunset porch at evening. At last Chillis reappeared and took a seat in one of them, quite in the usual way. He had been away, he said, attending to some business.

"An' I have fixed that matter all right about the boy's schoolin'," he added. "The papers are made out in the clerk's office an' will be sent to you as soon as they are recorded. There are five hundred and forty acres, which you will know how to manage better than I can tell you. You can sell by and by, ef you can't get the money out of it any other way. The taxes won't be much, the land being unimproved."

"You do not mean that you have *deeded* all your land to Willie?" asked Mrs. Smiley. "I protest against it: he must not have it! Would you let us rob you?" she asked wonderingly. "What are *you* to do, by and by, as you say?"

"Me? I shall do well enough. Money is o' no use to me. But ef I should want a meal or a blanket that I couldn't get, the boy wouldn't see me want them long. Ef he forgot old Joe Chillis, his mother wouldn't, I reckon."

"You pay too high a price for our remembrance, Mr. Chillis; we are not worth it. But why do you talk of forgetting? You are not going away from us?"

"Yes; I am goin' to start tomorrow for my old stampin' ground, east o' the mountains. My only livin' son is over there, somewhar. He don't amount to much—the Indian in him is too strong, but, like enough, he will be glad to see his father afore I die. An' I want to git away from here."

"You will come back? Promise me you will come back?" For something in his voice and his settled expression of melancholy and renunciation made her fear he was taking this step for a reason that could not be named between them.

"It is likely," he said, "but ef I come or no, don't fret about me. Just remember this that I am tellin' you now. The day I first saw you was the most fortunate day of my life. Ef I hadn't a-met you, I should have died as I had lived—like a creature without a soul. An' now I have a soul, in you. An' when I come to die, as I shall before many years, I shall die happy, thinkin' how my old hands had served the sweetest woman under heaven, and how they had been touched by hers so kindly, many a time, when she condescended to serve *me*."

What could she say to a charge like this? Yet say something she must, and so she answered, that he thought too highly of her, who was no better than other women, but that, since in his great singleness of heart, he did her this honor, to set her above all the world, she could only be humbly grateful and wish really to be what in his vivid imagination she seemed to him. Then she turned the talk upon less personal topics, and Willie was called and informed of the loss he was about to sustain, upon which there was a great deal of childish questioning and boyish regret for the good times no more to be that summer.

"I should like to take care of your boat," said he, "your hunting boat, I mean. If I had it over here, I would take Mamma down to it every Saturday, and she could sew and do everything there, just as she does at home, and it would be gay now, wouldn't it?"

"The old boat is sold, my boy; that an' the rowboat and the pony, too. You'll have to wait till I come back for huntin' and fishin' and ridin'."

Then Mrs. Smiley knew almost certainly that this visit was the last she would ever receive from Joe Chillis, and though she tried hard to seem unaffected by the parting and to talk of his return

162

hopefully, the effort proved abortive, and conversation flagged. Still he sat there silent and nearly motionless through the whole evening, thinking what thoughts she guessed only too well. With a great sigh, at last he rose to go.

"You will be sure to write at the end of your journey, and let us know how you find things there, and when you are coming back?"

"I will write," said he, "an' I want you to write back and tell me that you remember what I advised you some time ago." He took her hands, folded them in his own, kissed them reverently, and turned away.

Mrs. Smiley watched him going down the garden walk, as she had watched him a year before, and noted how slow and uncertain his steps had grown since then. At the gate he turned and waved his hand, and she in turn fluttered her little white handkerchief. Then she sat down with the handkerchief over her head and sobbed for a full five minutes.

"There are things in life one cannot comprehend," she muttered to herself, "things we cannot dare to meddle with or try to alter; providences, I suppose, they are. If God had made a man like that for me, of my own age, and given him opportunities suited to his capacities, and he had loved me as this man loves, what a life ours would have been!"

The summer weather and bracing northwest breezes from the ocean renewed, in a measure, Mrs. Smiley's health and restored her cheerful spirits, and, if she missed her old friend, she kept silent about it, as she did about most things that concerned herself. To Willie's questioning she gave those evasive replies children are used to receiving, but she frequently told him, in talks about his future, that Mr. Chillis had promised to send him to college, and that as long as he lived he must love and respect so generous a friend. "And, Willie," she never failed to add, "if ever you see an old man who is in need of anything—food, or clothes, or shelter—be very sure that you furnish them, as far as you are able." She was teaching him to pay his debt. "For, inasmuch as ye have done it unto the least of these," he had done it unto his benefactor.

September came, and yet no news had arrived from beyond the mountains. Captain Rumway's house was finished up to the last touch of varnish. The lawn and the shrubbery and fence were all just as they should be, yet, so far as anybody knew, no mistress had been provided for them, when, one warm and hazy afternoon, Mrs. Smiley received an invitation to look at the completed mansion and pass her judgment upon it.

"I am going to furnish it in good style," said its master, rather vauntingly, Mrs. Smiley thought, "and I hoped you would be so good as to give me your assistance in making out a list of the articles required to fit the house up perfectly, from parlor to kitchen."

"Any lady can furnish a list of articles for each room, Mr. Rumway, more or less costly, as you may order, but only the lady who is to live in the house can tell you what will please *her.*" And she smiled the very shadow of a superior smile.

Mr. Rumway had foolishly thought to get his house furnished according to Mrs. Smiley's taste, and now found he should have to consult Mrs. Rumway's, present or prospective, and the discovery annoyed him. Yet, why should he be annoyed? Was not the very opportunity presented that he had desired, of renewing his proposal to her to take the establishment in charge? So, although it compelled him to change his programme, he accepted the situation, and seized the tide at flood.

"It is that lady—the one I entreat to come and live in it—whose wishes I now consult. Once more will you come?"

Mrs. Smiley, though persistently looking aside, had caught the eloquent glance of the Captain's dark eyes, and something of the warmth of his face was reflected in her own. But she remained silent, looking at the distant highlands without seeing them.

"You must have seen," he continued, "that notwithstanding your former answer, I have been bold enough to hope you might change your mind, for, in everything I have done here, I have tried to follow your expressed wishes. I should in all else strive to make you as happy as by accepting this home you would make me. You do not answer; shall I say it is 'yes?'" He bent so close that his dark mop of hair just brushed her golden braids, and gave her a little shock like electricity, making her start away with a blush.

"Will you give me time to decide upon my answer, Mr. Rumway?"

"You asked for time before," he replied, in an agitated voice, "and, after making me suffer a week of suspense, refused me."

"I know it," she said simply, "and I was sorry I had asked it, but my reasons are even more imperative than they were then for wishing to delay. I want to decide right, at last," she added, with a faint attempt at a smile.

"That will be right which accords with your feelings, and certainly you can tell me now what they are—whether you find me the least bit lovable or not."

The gray eyes flashed a look up into the dark eyes, half of mirth and half of real inquiry. "I think one might learn to endure you, Mr. Rumway," she answered, demurely. "But," changing her manner, "I can not tell you whether or not I can marry you, until—until—well," she concluded desperately, "it may be a day or a week or a month. There is something to be decided, and until it is decided, I can not give an answer."

Captain Rumway looked very rebellious.

"I do not ask you to wait, Mr. Rumway," said Mrs. Smiley, tormentingly. "Your house need not be long without a mistress."

"Of course, I must wait, if you give me the least ground of hope. This place was made for you, and no other woman shall ever come into it as my wife—that I swear. If you will not have me, I will sell it and live a bachelor."

Mrs. Smiley laughed softly and tunefully. "Perhaps you would prefer to limit your endurance and tell me how long you *will* allow me to deliberate before you sell and retire to bachelorhood?"

"You know very well," he returned, ruefully, "that I shall always be hoping against all reason that the wished-for answer was coming at last."

"Then we will say no more about it at present."

"And I may come occasionally to learn whether that 'something' has been decided?"

"Yes, if you have the patience for it. But, I warn you, there is a chance of my having to say 'No.'"

"If there is only a chance of your having to say 'No,' I think I may incur the risk," said Rumway, with a sudden accession of hopefulness, and, as they walked home together once more, the gossips pronounced it an engagement. The Captain himself felt that it was, although, when he reviewed the conversation, he discovered that he founded his impression upon that one glance of the gray eyes rather than upon anything that had been said. And Mrs. Smiley put the matter out of mind as much as possible and waited.

One day, about the last of the month, a letter came to her from over the mountains. It ran in this wise:

> My lovely lady: I am once more among the familyar seanes of forty years ago. My son is hear, an' about as I expected. I had rather be back at Clatsop, with the old bote, but, owin' to circumstances I can't controll, I think it better to end my dais on this side ov the mountains. You need not look for me to come back, but I send you an' the boy my best love, an' hope you hav done as I advised.
>
> Yours, faithfully, til deth,
> Joe Chillis

Soon after the receipt of this letter, Captain Rumway called to inquire concerning the settlement of the matter on which his marriage depended. That evening he stayed later than usual, and, in a long confidential talk that he had with Mrs. Smiley, learned that there was a condition attached to the consummation of his wishes, which required his recognition of the claims of "poor old Joe" to be considered a friend of the family. To do him justice, he yielded the point more gracefully than, from his consciousness of his own position, could have been expected.

The next day, Mrs. Smiley wrote as follows:

> DEAR MR. CHILLIS: I shall move into the new house about the last of October, according to your advice. We—that is, myself, and Willie, and the present owner of the house— shall be delighted if you will come and stay with us. But if you decide to remain with your son, believe that we think of you very often and very affectionately, and wish you every possible happiness. R. agrees with me that the land ought to be deeded back to you, and I think you had best return and get the benefit of it. It would make you very comfortable for life, properly managed, and about that we might help you. Please write and let us know what to do about it.
>
> Yours affectionately,
ANNIE SMILEY

No reply ever came to this letter, and, as it was written ten years ago, Mrs. Rumway has ceased to expect any. Willie is about to enter college.